The Chronicles of Thumpus Wumpus

by

Carol Riddell &
Roy Chillingworth

A book for children (especially between 8 and 13), the text was previously published by Harper Collins, Australia under their Angus and Robertson imprint, now long out of print.
This edition published by Amazon Create Space,
Illustrations by Roy Chillingworth
Text by Carol Riddell

The Chronicles of Thumpus Wumpus

1.
An Introduction.

Long ago and far away there was a tiny village. If you stood on a hill above the village you would see that you were on the edge of a great forest. It stretched as far as the eye could see, rising towards distant snow-capped mountains, hazy in the sunlight. In the other direction, the land dropped away slowly, a mix of woods and open spaces with chimney smoke marking occasional villages. There were even towns down near the coast, but they were too far away to see.

The few people who knew about the village called it 'the village in between', because it was between the wilderness of the forest and the inhabited lands below. No road led to it; if you wanted to get there you had to walk, or ride on horseback. Not many people visited.

The villagers lived a simple life. They cut a few trees to build their log houses and collected fallen logs to heat their wood stoves. In the clearing they had made they kept goats for milk and hens for eggs. They grew vegetables and some corn. There were beehives, and the forest provided them with berries and mushrooms, herbs and roots to eat. They made earthenware pots and plates from local clay. Anything else they needed, they traded for down the hill. On the whole, they were content. They did not spend much time down the hill where were more people, or up the hill in the wilderness. Just keeping alive was hard enough work.

In the forest lived the usual animals that live in forests. But there was one extra. He was a *Thumpus Wumpus* and that was his name as well. He was as big as a Highland cow, and even more hairy, with shaggy brown fur which was always getting twigs caught in it. He had a long, powerful tail - his thumpus, with which he could make a loud booming noise when he bashed it on the ground or against large trees - his wumpus. When he was happy - especially at nightfall or when the moon was full - he would howl (*he* called it singing), a dreadful, long drawn out gargling noise, followed by the wump of his thumpus. He was a very rare animal - so rare that he himself had never seen another Thumpus since he was a cub.

The villagers were very frightened of this racket, though the most they ever saw of Thumpus was a shadow far away through the trees. They imagined there were many Thumping Wumpii - they called them 'Thumps' and thought they were very ferocious. Apart from two daring young hunters we shall meet later, they never went far into the forest, and only in daytime at that.

In actual fact, Thumpus Wumpus was a pretty harmless sort of animal. He scruffled around in the woods, sniffling at anything, eating what he could find - as long as it didn't bite back. He had a placid and easygoing disposition. True, he was a bit devious and, if hungry, might sneak up on a potential meal from the other side of a tree to catch it from behind. He also smelt rather rancid.

The special thing about Thumpus was that he was *telepathic.* He could pick up the thoughts and feelings of other animals and project his own thoughts to them. It was his main means of defence against the more ferocious animals that lived in some parts of the forest, for whom he would have made a tasty meal.

Although the villagers were frightened of Thumpus, he was interested in them. His telepathic sense caught scraps of thought from the village. At first, they made him confused and ill. But, perhaps because he was so lonely, instead of clearing off, far from thought range of the village, he continued to listen till he began to understand. He even practised sending small thoughts like, <Fungi tasty this week>, or, <Feels good to have a full tummy.> After a while he became quite good at it.

As you can see, Thumpus was ready for closer contact with human kind, and this is how it happened.

<u>Scientific Note.</u>

Thumpus Wumpus is the only remaining species of the ancient order, Scrofulus Woofulus, other varieties being long extinct. Characterised by patching and moulting of their dishevelled, shaggy fur (Scrofulous) and by the ghastly sounds they emitted (Woofulus), they existed briefly at the dawn of history. It has been surmised that they used their telepathic faculty to keep order in the forests, but this theory is contested by Crutt (q.v.), who thinks they were merely an aberration.

The Chronicles of Thumpus Wumpus

2.
Meeting

One fine morning, when the forest was damp and tangy with smells of autumn, the birches were yellowing slightly in the glades and the pine trees had vague thoughts of cold, long nights to come, two children came out to gather mushrooms in the woods beyond the clearing surrounding the village. They were happy in the autumn sunshine, smelling the autumn smells, listening to the occasional autumn squawk of the woodland birds. Tash was ten, and dark like his mother. Tesh was twelve and fair like her father. They knew about wild mushrooms as well as anyone in the village; which were good to eat, which were better left alone, and those few types which should *never* on any account be picked. With them they did not make mistakes, for just one taste could spell serious trouble - or even disaster.

There were plenty of mushrooms in the forest, but today they were after a specially tasty variety - large, with a round brown top, whitish, sponge-like gills and a fat stalk touched with black lines - the famous 'gurgli', delicious in soups, and to be dried for the winter. There weren't so many of these mushrooms at the edge of the forest so it was tempting to venture a little further in, to glades of birch deeper amid the pines, which they had visited before only in more experienced company. This they should not have done; there had been clear warnings of the multiple dangers of venturing too far into the trees, of getting lost, of wild animals that might be hungry, and especially of the secretive 'Thumps' who, as far as anyone knew, might relish a young human as a morning snack.

Nothing was further from the mind of old, grey-muzzled Thumpus as he sat, satisfied but a little lonely, and enjoyed the morning. He began to distinguish the thoughts and feelings of Tash and Tesh as they wandered the woods on the trail of elusive gurgli. He knew that they wanted to take full baskets back to please their parents; that they loved the autumn feel of the place almost as much as he did; they were *really* happy.

Not far from where Thumpus sat was a clearing with a small stream, around the edge of which were growing large numbers of gurgli, so far undiscovered by humans. It was about a quarter of an hour's wander deeper into the woods than where Tash and Tesh were searching.

Then Thumpus did something *he* should not have done, something that was to change his life and that of the children, for ever. True, it did not seem to be dangerous. Humans, being much less sensitive than animals, could only pick up the vaguest feelings from his telepathic sendings. Nevertheless, he was usually careful. But the morning was so nice, the sunshine so mellow, the enjoyment of the children in his forest so delightful, that he forgot himself for a moment and projected an image of the gurgli in the glade nearby.

Tesh shook her head. In it was a picture of a woodland glade not a long way further into the forest, covered with unspoilt, fresh gurgli, some of them almost as large as a dinner plate. She had picked up Thumpus' projection perfectly! Tash, however, had just got a feeling, - <Mushrooms!> and some excitement.

'Tash, I know where we can fill our baskets with gurgli! I saw it in my head, absolutely clear. It's not far away in that direction,' said Tesh, pointing deeper into the forest. 'There's a sort of clearing, with a stream flowing through it and there are masses and masses of them!'

Tash thought of the endlessness of the forest, of how easy it was to get lost, of parental warnings, and of trust in him to be sensible. But he did not want to appear faint-hearted to his sister.

'Well,' he said, doubtfully, 'we'll go a little way, but we must be really careful to remember the way we came from here.' He was fairly sure he could find his way back from their present spot.

Following Tesh's lead, they moved deeper into the woods, climbing slightly, till all the little signs they used to find their way - the form the roots of a particular tree took, the way the trees bunched together, variations in the undergrowth - became unfamiliar. Still Tesh went on, following the image in her head, turning this way and that to avoid trees and dead branches, till Tash felt more and more worried. However, there was nothing he could do but follow Tesh.

In a quite short time - to anxious Tash it seemed much longer - they entered a glade; it was not really a clearing, but a place where the trees were not so dense, where more birches grew, and where the sunlight dappled the ground in an endless patchwork of different shapes. And amongst them all, gurgli! - the crop of a lifetime; something to be recalled round the winter fire for years to come; an endless supply of pure, unadulterated gurgli, far more than they could ever carry home.

Tesh and Tash set to to fill their baskets, anxieties forgotten, oblivious to everything but gurgli.

'You see, I was right. They *are* here.'

'You were right,' Tash had to admit.

There were so many mushrooms, the children could even be choosy, picking only the freshest, largest, most perfectly formed specimins. It wasn't long before the baskets were overflowing. They sat by the little stream enjoying the abundance of harvest.

'This isn't the River, is it,' said Tesh. The River was the name of the large stream that flowed by the village and gave them water.

'No, it's much too tiny. Besides, I think it flows in the other direction.' Tash did not want to admit that he was not sure exactly where the River was. All his anxieties were returning now that the excitement of the gurgli picking was over.

'Tash,' whispered Tesh, leaning over to him, 'something is watching us!'

Thumpus, who had been cautiously peering at the children round the side of a tree at the edge of the glade, picked up the thought behind the words perfectly and hastily drew his head back.

'Damn!' he thought.

'It doesn't want to be discovered,' Tesh went on, cuddling up to the now dejected Tash. All their pleasure at the wonderful harvest of gurgli had evaporated. The morning was no longer bright. They were frightened and alone in the sinister forest of the stories they had heard.

'We've got to get back home,' said Tash. He clenched his teeth. He was not sure where home was. How long had they been in the glade? Where had the sun been when they arrived? He stood up, picked up his laden basket and started off in the direction he thought they should go, more or less following the stream downhill. Tesh followed.

'Are you sure that's the right way?' objected Tesh, mildly. 'I thought we came over the ridge to get here.' Tash was not sure. Nor was he sure if Tesh was right.

'I *think* its this way.'

Thumpus was suddenly very awake. The children were heading in the wrong direction, on a path that would never bring them back to the village.

'Damn!' he thought again, 'and blast, too!'

'The thing's there again,' said Tesh, misinterpreting the thought this time. 'It doesn't want us to go.'

'So it can eat us, probably!' Tash started to run.

Thumpus felt woolly in his head. What should he do? They were heading away from the village and Kamal, the ever-hungry bear, might find them if they went much further, especially after dark. He could leave them to their fate, but - he had been responsible for sending the thought which had drawn the children to the glade in the first place. Tesh had picked up that thought as no human had ever done before. Besides, he *liked* these children. He had never dared to be so close to humans and he was finding them were more than intriguing - they were positively attractive. On the other hand, if he did do something to help them, they would learn who he was; people might come after him from the village and he would have to leave the area.

Thumpus wumped his tail on the ground in frustration, snapping a small tree and sending a deep boom echoing through the forest. The terrified children panicked and ran, scattering mushrooms behind them. Back in the village, people looked at each other, startled at the unexpected sound on the sunny morning, and Tash and Tesh's parents grabbed sticks. Shouting to others for help, they started for the woods.

The sound penetrated the wool in Thumpus' head. He had to *do* something, *now*.

He loped around, on a course to merge with that of the fleeing children. When he had to, he could be surprisingly fast.

<Stop!> he sent, <Wrong way! I'll help you.> Tesh pulled up short. She had received the projection loud and clear.

'Tash, there's something wants to help us. We're going the wrong way. It called to us. I heard it, clearly - in my head.'

Part of Tash just wanted to run and run, but he couldn't leave his sister behind. That would be the end of everything. He stopped and reluctantly returned to where she was standing, rooted to the spot.

Fearfully they looked around, and there, suddenly, lumbering between the trees and stopping as soon as it saw them, was a huge, mangy beast with an enormous tail and a long pink tongue hanging out of its large jaws.

'This is it,' thought Tash. 'The End! If only we hadn't gone off to get the gurgli. If only I hadn't listened to Tesh!'

<Friend!> sent Thumpus, in spite of himself. These were the most unlikely friends he could imagine. Besides, he didn't have any friends, *ever*. <Won't eat you.>
Tesh stared at the dishevelled monster with wide eyes.

'That's what's talking to me!' Her breath came unevenly. 'He won't hurt us. *He wants to be friends*.' Tash didn't hear the sending like Tesh, but he felt better. The fear was suddenly his own and not the situation's.

The little group eyed each other cautiously. Thumpus saw, for the first time, the bright, intelligent, frightened eyes of the small humans, looked into them - and was hooked like a fish on a line. They *were* important, the most important thing that had ever happened to him. He felt his heart turn over and a giddy shiver went right through him. He *loved*. He raised his head and gave a soft, whining yowl, like a dying pig. He sat down on the ground. This felt awful.

Tesh and Tash saw, for the first time, the large, soft, silly, slightly duplicitous brown eyes of a Thumpus Wumpus. They were irresistible.

'He's gorgeous,' breathed Tesh, 'so cuddly. And what a mess!' She thought of herself combing that matted brown and cream fur, disentangling bits of stick and bark, even of being licked by the dangling pink tongue.

'You could ride on his back,' said Tash, finally releasing his fear.
Far away, in the direction they hadn't been running - the direction of the village - came the shouts of searchers and worried parents.

Overcome with a new wisdom, Thumpus, got up and turned.

<This way,> he sent, <Lead you back.>

He lumbered off between the trees, slowly, dejectedly. Now he would have to lose them again, just found. How could he bear it?

Tesh, too, found a new wisdom in herself.

<We'll meet you again, just here. You'll lead us to you.> She thought the thought and at the same time, sent it.

Thumpus received it, like a bell clanging in his head. For the first time since he parted from his mother, someone had sent a message personally directed to *him*. He started shivering again. This was getting totally out of control.

<All right,> he answered. <Know when you coming. Will call.>

'Tash, he'll meet us again. He says so, inside!'

But the anxious voices of human adults were getting louder, and nearer.

'Tash! Tesh! Where are you? Come back - at once!'

Thumpus moved to one side and melted into the trees like a patch of light and shade. The children ran towards the voices. The worried, scolding arms of their parents embraced them. Somebody saw a moving shadow at the edge of vision.

'Why were you so far away? Thank God you're all right. There's a thump about. Didn't you hear it wumping? You could have been eaten!'

'But-,' began Tesh.

'No buts. Lord's Mercy, we found you safe! Back to the village.'

The gurgli lay scattered around the forest where they had been dropped in the panic. One or two remained in the baskets, the only evidence of the glade and the day's adventures.

Thumpus felt more dejected and confused than he could ever remember. What on earth had he got himself into? What had happened to him? It was crazy to meet Tash and Tesh again. The villagers would kill him if they saw him with them. He absent-mindedly chewed on some grass to settle his stomach.

The Chronicles of Thumpus Wumpus

3.
Secret Rendezvous

Of course, their stories about meeting the wump were not believed. Even less were Tesh's assertions that it was friendly and that she could talk with it 'in her head'. That made her mother angry.

'What rubbish! Are you sick, girl? Animals can't talk, in your head or outside. How can we let you out alone if you're going to come up with such stories?' Even their friends scoffed in disbelief. The children were forbidden to go to the woods alone, and that, for several days, was that.

But Tash and Tesh knew that they were not making it up At least they were both sure about meeting Thumpus and how he had led them back towards the village. Tash had heard no voices in his head, and tried to persuade Tesh that she had imagined that bit - at least to compromise with parental views.

'But he *did* talk to me. Otherwise how would we have found the gurgli or known that he was friendly?' Tesh was not quite sure how it had happened, though. She would wake up at night, thinking about it. Surely it was not some dream. She *had* had the pictures in her head. She had sent one and the wump had understood.

As for Thumpus, he thought it was the most miserable time of his whole life. He had messed *everything* up. The children were gone and would no doubt never be allowed out alone again. His peace of mind was gone. The pleasant, lonely life scruffling around in the woods had no appeal any more. Life was just *miserable*.

For a whole week he resisted doing anything. Then it was just too much. In spite of himself and fearing the worst, he was driven by feelings he did not understand and could not control. In the woods with the children, love had woken in his heart. He just wanted to be with them.

The night was star spangled, with a quarter moon. He crept down through the forest, close to the village clearing. To Tesh, who could hear him, he sent a despairing call:

<Unhappy! Miss you so much. Come see again.> Tesh was dreaming of the monster beast. In her dream, it had crawled up to her abjectly and was licking her toes with its pink tongue.

'Good beast,' she said absently and half woke. As she did so, she heard Thumpus' dejected message. In an instant, she was wide awake. Another instant and she was by Tash's bed on the other side of the room.

'Tash, Tash!' she whispered urgently. 'Wake up! He's calling us. He's unhappy. He misses us. He wants to see us again.' Tash, awakened abruptly from his own dreams, lay still with wide open eyes, looking at the starlight softened dark of the room. He was fed up with being disbelieved by his parents. He felt rebellious and defiant.

'Come on then, let's go to him,' he said, and instantly regretted it. But the words were spoken. Tesh needed only that encouragement from her brother. Silently, they put coats over their night things. Silently, they picked up their shoes. Almost silently, they opened the creaking door and crept out. Another door and they were with the stars outside. No one had stirred!

<We're coming. Wait for us,> sent Tesh and once more Thumpus heard her message loud in his head. They headed to the edge of the sleeping village and across the cleared area to the wall of dark woodland blackening the sky.

As they approached the trees, they paused, scared again.

'Suppose he's fooling us,' Tash said, softly. 'Suppose he just wanted to lure us out here in the dark, alone, so he could eat us undisturbed!' Tesh shivered.

'He won't do that,' she replied. 'He just wants to see us. He's lonely.' As they stood, undecided, in front of the line of trees marking the beginning of the endless forest, she sent another message into nothingness:

<We're frightened. What do you want with us. Do you want to eat us?> Thumpus, heading along the edge of the woods in the general direction he thought the children might arrive - if they really came at all - was also feeling anxious. Would they come alone? Might there not be villagers creeping up behind them? But the ambience of the village seemed calm, full of night sleep and dream states. When Tesh'-s message came to him, he realised he was already very close - 20 metres inside the tree line, almost opposite to where they were.. How could anyone be frightened of a Thumping Wumpus? Such a delightful, soft, shambling creature. They must know he would never hurt them. He wasn't a Mountain Lion or a Grizzly Bear. He made a quick telepathic check to be quite sure that the thoughts of such a beast weren't anywhere in the vicinity and sent a message back to Tesh.

<Friend. Hurt *never*! Want be with again! Close in woods.>

'He's there,' whispered Tesh, very quietly. 'He says he'll never hurt us, that he's our friend.' She pulled at Tash's sleeve to go to the woods' edge. Tash hesitated.

'How do we know he's truthful,' he thought, remembering the friendly, captivating, slight duplicity in the eyes he had seen in their first encounter a week before. But he allowed Tesh to pull him forward to the trees.

In the dark in front of them, there was a darker patch - a patch that moved.

<Friend, friend, friend!> sent Thumpus, picking up their fear, rapidly mounting to terror as his dark, uncertain

shape slowly approached them. An incredible feeling suddenly swept over him. They had come - to *him*! Not for any other reason. Just because he was Thumpus. The urge to howl and wump was almost overwhelming. But Thumpus had some sense in him and knew it would spoil everything because it would wake the village. However,the feelings were so strong he couldn't stand up any longer, and dropped on to his belly, panting breaths shaking him.

Summoning more courage than she knew she had, Tesh moved slowly towards him, Tash a little behind. Lord, it was large! Even lying on the ground, the dark, barely distinguishable shape was almost as high as she was. If the images in her head were wrong, they were wump meat! She was less than 2 metres away from him! She stopped, and hesitatingly put out her hand. The only thing Thumpus could think of to do was to edge forward and lick it , gently, sweetly.

Tesh shook with suppressed excitement. Just like in her dream.

'He licked me!' The words burst out of her in a low voice. 'Tash, he licked me - it's rough, like wet sandpaper!' Nervously, Tash advanced to his sister and put his hand gingerly forward. Once more, Thumpus obliged.

'Wow! You could plane wood with that tongue.' Thumpus picked up the thought behind the words, and was a little hurt. His soft, tentative tongue, licking like a baby Wumpus at his mother's nipple, compared to - Thumpus was not clear what sandpaper or planes were, but he sensed they were rough. Meanwhile, Tesh, confident now that her dream had been confirmed, stepped forward and started to run her hand over the thick, woolly, matted fur.

'He's so soft.'

'But he smells pretty strong,' countered Tash, nevertheless himself advancing and running his hand over and through Thumpus' protection against the winter, now beginning to grow strong and thick.

'We could wash him, and comb him.' Thumpus, in seventh heaven as the children stroked and cuddled him, had a dreadful thought - Getting to know these children wasn't going to be all pleasure. He *didn't* smell. His coat was perfectly all right as it was. It had served him for many years without being washed.

<Don't smell,> he sent out querulously.

'He says he doesn't smell' said Tesh. <I'm afraid you do, my dear,> she sent back, <rather dreadfully, actually.>

'They say people can't smell their own smell,' said Tash. 'Probably he's been on his own for years and wump smell just seems like 'no-smell' to him.' Thumpus became aware that loving and being loved had a definite down side. People judged you all the time. He changed tack, giving just the tiniest little whine. The sound was like someone dragging a knife across rusty wire. The children shrank back a little.

<Hush, you'll wake the whole village!> sent Tesh, after a moment to recover. Then she realised the poor wump had not meant to be loud and stroked her fingers once more though his fur.

<You two smell,> he sent, <not me. You pong> - he couldn't resist fighting back a bit - <like pine needles on summer morning.>

'Oh, he says we smell, too, but lovely like fresh pine needles.' Tesh giggled. She didn't care much about the wump's bodyodour. That could be dealt with later - though the appalling breath would be more difficult. Perhaps they could change his diet. She turned her attention to the hulking animal once more.

<Tell us about you. Who are you? What are you?>

<Thumpus Wumpus, of course,> returned Thumpus, <of Thumping Wumpii. Perhaps last one,> he added, sadly.

Tesh was shocked. Like all the villagers, she had thought the woods were full of Thumps.

<What about your mother and father? Your brothers and sisters?>

<Don't know father. Brothers, sisters, no - only me. Wumpii leave mums as get older - just way we're made. Maybe dead now.> Thumpus paused. <Happy to have friends,> he added. Tesh shared his story with Tash. Both of them hugged the old beast hard. He shivered and was sad for a moment, remembering all the years of loneliness, all the years without any other Wumpii around.

'We've got to go back.' Tash had suddenly remembered what they had done. 'It'll be morning soon. We've got to get in before anyone wakes.' Tesh knew he was right.

'We must meet him again, soon, for longer, in daylight. This way isn't any good. We'll have to find a way for everyone to meet him and learn that he's gentle, not violent.'

<You aren't violent, ever, are you?> she sent to Thumpus.

<*Never*!> returned Thumpus, not even thinking about mice and wood hares he killed occasionally to supplement his diet.

<We must go,> sent Tesh. <But we'll see again very soon, in daytime. Don't worry, listen for my thought. Have to find a way to introduce you to the others, so not afraid of you.>

'Bye now!' Tesh and Tash cuddled up to the huge, fawning beast as if they had known him all their lives, suffered another lick, and ran off out of the trees across the cleared land, as the sky gave just the slightest hint that another day might be in store for them. They got back into their room without incident, flung off their coats and snuggled, chilled, to warm themselves in the bedclothes.

After a while, Thumpus got up, turned, and retreated slowly into his forest. They were wonderful, he thought, sharp and responsive; but *so* critical. Thumpus' sense of self was somewhat mauled. Did he really smell? Was his tongue so rough? Did even his tiniest whine sound so loud? Yet it was so lovely to have them touch him, stroke him, to have friends at last.

For the next couple of days and nights, the forest resounded with wumps and howls as Thumpus released his joyful feelings. The villagers shook their heads and did not go alone into the woods. But, at Tash and Teshs' house, something was going on.

The Chronicles of Thumpus Wumpus

4.
Discovered!

Lelesh, the children's mother, looked in on her sleeping brood just after 7.30. The sun was shining, a glorious day, and the children were usually well up by this time, since everyone went to bed pretty early in the village. The first thing she noticed was the smell. There was a very strong animal smell in the room, somewhat reminiscent of goat. Then she saw the outdoor coats, thrown carelessly on the floor and, bending down, she traced the source of the smell to them. Next, as she bent over the sleeping Tesh, she realised that the smell also came from her face and hair. The same applied to Tash. Finally, she left the room quietly and sought her husband, Prush, just getting up in the other room.

'Something very strange, Prush,' she said. 'I want you to come to the children's room for a moment.'

Prush pulled on his shirt and trousers and dutifully followed his wife back into the children's room.

'Do you notice anything,' she whispered.

'Funny stink - like a goat, I would say. The children are sleeping late.'

'Look at the coats. They've been out last night. We've got to get to the bottom of this!'

Prush went over to the now restless Tash and gently shook his shoulder. Tash and Tesh were his pride and joy.

'Wake up, Son,' he said. Tash gave a shiver and emerged into the bright morning, stretching.

'Tired.' He yawned, then realised that both his parents were in the room. 'Something the matter?' By now, Tesh was stirring as well.

'What's the stink in here? You two been out with the goats last night?'

'No,' said Tash, truthfully, 'of course not' - this for emphasis. He was still a little confused from sleep.

'Yes, we were,' lied his sister, who had become fully awake while attention was on her brother, and, taking in the situation with parents and coats, and a definite smell in the room, realised that the game was up. Maybe goats would save them!

'Goats!' Her mother turned on her sharply. 'What's this all about. You've been cuddling up to them from the stink on you!' She wrinkled her nose. 'And it isn't quite goat smell either. Now, we'd better get to the bottom of this - and fast. It could be dangerous at night. No-one goes out alone. Besides, you two are banned from going out alone at all right now!'

Tash and Tesh glanced at each other. They hadn't thought of preparing a story in case of discovery, and their first responses had made it clear to their parents that something was certainly amiss. Tesh suddenly realised that she was sensing her parents' mood - there was more anxiety than anger, but it was unstable.

'It was a dare,' she said, hoping to take the pressure off Tash. 'I dared Tash to go out in the moonlight, and he took me up on it. We were fed up with being kept in,' she added. This seemed a good stratagem, to turn some of the responsibility back on her parents.

'Yes, that's right,' said Tash, lamely, following his sister's lead, and contradicting his own first words. 'She dared me, and we went out to see the goats.' His slight hesitation made it clear to Lelesh that the truth was not coming out. At least not all of it.

'Now tell me,' she spoke slowly, in a voice that said the children had better not mess with her, 'what's going on. I don't like you trying to fool us with stories. You're transparent as two glass windows. It was Tash that told thc truth, at first, wasn't it?' She glared accusingly at Tesh.

Tesh could sense a tinge of anger in her mother's anxious feelings now. 'We've had it,' she thought. 'She's even noticed that it's not goat smell.' The only thing left was to try to play it out and hope for some diversion.

'I did dare Tash to go out,' she answered. At least that was more or less truthful.

'And where; and why?' Her father's thoughts were actually anxious and loving, though his voice was stern.

'For an adventure,' she said, 'to the wood's edge.' In another situation, that would perhaps have been all right, earning them no more than a good talking to $\frac{1}{2\pi}$ but they hadn't explained the smell. And she knew her mother wouldn't let up.

At that moment, the diversion she had hoped for happened, but the worst one possible in the circumstances. In remembering his pleasure at the night's meeting, Thumpus emitted a howling whoop and wumped his tail magnificently against a big old pine tree. Even he was gratified by the result.

'Eegh - Oww - Aargh - Ugh - Grrrr -' *Thwack!* The noise resounded through the woods and spread over the village. Lelesh and Prush blenched and shuddered. Tesh and Tash looked at each other. Tesh clearly felt Thumpus' joy and knew he was happy to have been with them. In spite of the circumstances, she could not totally repress a little smirk and half giggle that bubbled up in her.

Lelesh's sharp eyes were focused on Tesh's face. She missed neither grin nor giggle. The cat or, in this case, Thumpus - was out of the bag!'

'I *knew* it,' she said, horrified. 'You've been out after that terrible thump. And by the smell of you, you got pretty close to it!'

'You can't be serious,' said Prush in a strangled voice. 'That thing would have had them in an instant.' There was no use dissembling any more. The children glanced at each other. It was Tash who now came to the fore.

'It's not an it - it's a *he*. His name's Thumpus.'

'He's not terrible at all,' he continued, the words tumbling out, 'he's lovely. He's lonely. He was so happy to meet us. We cuddled up to him. He does speak to Tesh in her thoughts. That's how we found him and knew that he was our friend. He's lovely,' he repeated, 'We want you to meet him.'

'That's right,' Tesh confirmed. 'You see, he *does* speak to me inside. I know everything he thinks, as he thinks it. He's lonely and friendly. There aren't any other Thumps. He's the only one. Nobody needs to be afraid of him. You've got to come and see him.'

It was the turn of Lelesh and Prush to look at each other. This was all too much to believe.

'You will stay indoors,' said Lelesh, sternly. 'You will not go out, day or night, except to the toilet hut. If you try, we will lock you in your room. In the meantime, we have to talk to Indalesh about this.' Prush nodded, reinforcing her decision.

Indalesh was the children's grandmother. She was aged, all wrinkles, but the people of the village venerated old people. Quite rightly, they felt that if one grew old, surviving accident and illness, one must have accumulated great wisdom and experience. Indalesh was respected by the whole village.

Lelesh and Prush were good parents. Although Tash and Tesh were not afraid of them, they resolved to obey the prohibition, at least for the time being. Thumpus seemed to be so happy at their meeting, Tesh thought, that perhaps he would not be impatient for another one. Maybe Indalesh would understand.

Lelesh and Prush went to see Indalesh and told them all that had happened as they saw it. How could they stop the children from being in touch with the ghastly thump? Indalesh looked at them in their fear, chewing on a sweet liquorish stick as she often did when she was thoughtful.

'Well, in spite of the stories, no one's every actually been killed by thumps,' she said, 'or even seen one properly, up to now.'

'What about the Karinish twins,' countered Prush. 'They went exploring over to the East and were never heard of again. Thumps were heard howling in that direction.'

Indalesh regarded him steadily.

'Maybe. But there's no proof. It could have been something else. The Death Bear, or something we don't know about away in the deep forest. From what the children say, the thumps could have been trying to warn the Karinishes.'

'How can we be sure?' Lelesh was still very worried. 'Everyone says thumps are dreadful. Even if what Tesh and Tash say *could* be true, it might just be fooling them, waiting for a good opportunity.'

'What better opportunity than alone at night in the forest? I need to talk to the children. By myself, I think.'

Indalesh did not hurry. The story would not be any less or more true if she rushed round, and maybe a night's sleep would calm things down. Lelesh had said they had promised to obey and not go out again. Let it cool a little.

Next morning, after breakfast, the autumn sun already warming the village, she hobbled round to the log house of Prush and Lelesh. It looked good in the sunlight, a curl of smoke coming from the chimney. Peaceful. Being a little deaf, she heard the occasional whoops and wumps from Thumpus, now getting less frequent anyway, only as background noise.

In their room, she affixed the children with her wise, still twinkly eyes, smiled at them, chewed her stick and waited for the story to come out. Tash and Tesh loved their Gran and respected her. They told her everything, every detail they could remember.

'He talks to you in your head?' Indalesh questioned Tesh again. This was the hardest part of the story to believe. 'But not to you.' she turned to Tash.

'I feel something. I don't get pictures. Still, I believe Tesh. Everything she says, happens.'

'He seems to get thoughts from both of us,' said Tesh. 'He understands everything I send quite clearly.'

'It has been heard of, very rarely- My own grandmother was supposed to have been able to know people's thoughts.' The second big question was - what were the animal's intentions? 'Now, do you really believe that this 'Thumpus' is not violent? Perhaps his secret intention is to eat you up.'

'No it isn't. He's our friend,' said Tash

'He's not violent at all. Not to us, not to the village. Not to anyone. He's a strange, lonely creature. He just wants to be friends - with everyone, I think,' Tesh added.

Indalesh hesitated. Part of her wanted to accept the children's story. Another part struggled with the beliefs of a lifetime. Thumps were common. Thumps were violent. Thumps would eat anyone caught out alone in the woods and in the past had been responsible for the deaths of some. She also knew the other villagers would not accept the word of the children alone.

'People will not believe this, even if it is true,' she said, after a long pause.

Tesh had a brilliant idea.

'Come with us then,' she urged her grandmother. 'We'll go and meet him. They'll believe *you*.'

'Do you think he would come to us, even during the day?'

'Yes, he would. We only went at night because we were forbidden to visit the forest in the daytime.'

In spite of her years, Indalesh felt a surge of excitement. It was like being a girl again. On the other hand, she was confused. What a risk! She believed the children; but what if she were wrong? Suppose the wump wanted to eat them all. Her loss wouldn't be so bad - she had had a good, long life. But the children - Yet again, if Tesh *could* communicate with it.... They'd have to keep it a secret. The rest of the villagers would never understand.

'I have a better idea,' she said, 'one that I might be able to convince your parents about. You can send it thoughts? From how far away?'

'I don't know,' admitted Tesh. 'If I concentrate, I think I can tell how he's feeling, even from here. I think he can feel me, too.'

'All right. You and your parents come to the edge of the wood. Send it a thought that I want to meet it and tell it to come close, close enough to be seen. I'll go forward and we'll see if it really is friendly.'

'We can come with you,' said Tash.

'Your parents would never allow that, but I might just persuade them to give it a try with me going forward alone. And you mustn't tell anyone else *at all* about this.'

If the wump would allow itself to be seen, went Indalesh's reasoning, then it proved that Tesh could talk to it. That supported the rest of the children's story. If so, she wouldn't be harmed if she went to the beast. A lot of 'ifs'. She gulped, but the children were nodding. She would try to win over Prush and Lelesh to the plan.

It turned out to be very hard work. Prush and Lelesh objected that it was too much risk, that Indalesh was indispensable to the village, that *they* would be responsible if they accepted and she was harmed. But Indalesh could be determined if she wanted (some people called it stubborn). She explained it all again and again. If the beast showed up when Tesh called it in her head, it already proved the major part of the story. If it didn't, nothing was lost. And Prush and Lelesh could arm themselves with big staves to drive the beast off, if it wasn't friendly. Eventually, over many protests, she had her way.

It rained later that day, a mushroom inducing rain. Among others of their kind, gurgli stirred and sprouted. It was an auspicious sign. The next morning, however, was fine and, after breakfast, the experiment was set to begin. Tesh could feel that Thumpus was still in the area and beginning to get over the euphoria of their first meeting. He wanted to see them again.

The little group went across the cleared land and just into the woods' edge. Prush and Lelesh carried strong staves, sharpened at one end. Everyone was nervous. From where they stood, they could see clearly about 60 metres into the woods in the morning sunlight. Now for the critical part. Would Thumpus come?

<Thumpus, dear,> sent Tesh, <are you there?>

Thumpus heard her call clearly. There was also an uneasy-making background of anxiety around her. Tash was there, too, he knew, but he could sense the presence of others as well.

<Can hear you,> he thought back, cautiously.

<We're at edge of wood. Come near, so we can see you. Our mum and dad here, Gran, too. Wants come and meet you.>

Thumpus was concerned. It could be a trick.

<I only want to be with you,> he sent.

'He says he only wants to be with us,' Tesh told the others. 'He's worried you want to hurt him.'

"Tell him it's the only way you can ever meet him again," said Indalesh, firmly.

<They're afraid of you,> sent Tesh. <They have to be sure you don't mean to hurt us - or them,> she added. <Won't let us see you again unless you agree.>

There was quite a long pause, while Thumpus tried to get his head round this. He was afraid of *them*, afraid they might hurt him. *They* killed things. Not him. No-one could be afraid of him. He never killed anything. Well, nothing big, anyway$\frac{1}{2\pi}$ But he did want to see Tash and Tesh again. Very much. His life was different now. He didn't think he could go on living without seeing them. So he had no choice, really.

<What to do?> he eventually replied, grudgingly.

Tesh's heart leapt. She was beginning to worry that he wouldn't respond.

<Come near enough so can just see you. Then let my Gran come meet you.>

<If must.> Thumpus began shambling from his position about half a kilometre away. He would not hurry. A stupid plan!

The others were getting more and more impatient at the wait. 'Probably it won't come near at all and we can forget this whole silly idea,' thought Lelesh.

Tesh spoke, briefly. 'He's coming!' Everybody waited. After a long while, a large shape emerged at the edge of their vision. Blending with the dapple of trees and sunshine, it seemed to be there one moment and gone the next.

<Come closer,> sent Tesh.

Cautiously Thumpus approached. He could sense them clearly enough and see them, too. At just 60 metres distance, he stopped. That was quite near enough. Anxiety levels were very high.

<Gurgli,> he sent, hopefully. A large gurgli was right where he had stopped. Tesh ignored the attempted diversion.

The adults were looking in some horror at the beast sitting on its haunches through the woods in front of them. They saw a big furry head, a long, lolloping tongue, big *teeth* and a matted coat, brown on top and cream-coloured under the body. And an enormous tail.

<My Gran, Indalesh, is going to come and say hello to you,> sent Tesh. <She old and lovely, wise. Won't hurt you.>

<If must,> responded Thumpus. He could see who Tesh meant. An aura of fear surrounded her. What was she afraid of? It was *he* who should be afraid.

Indalesh clenched her hands and made herself release them. The beast had come, in response to Tesh's call. That meant it ought, probably, *ought* to be OK..

Tash and Tesh were looking at her in admiration. Prush and Lelesh seemed to be in shock at the events. Summoning more courage than she knew she had, she started forward. Adventure, be blowed! She was too old for this sort of thing.

Nearer and nearer she came to Thumpus. Fear approached fear. Suddenly from somewhere deep inside, Thumpus felt, 'This old lady's not going to hurt me.' From behind her fear, he sensed what Tesh had sent. She was wise and loving. Somebody it could be really nice to know. He relaxed.

A lovely, warm feeling of acceptance flowed through Indalesh, smothering her fear. She approached the beast, noticing its big, diffident, reassuring, brown eyes. She held out her hand. Slowly, Thumpus reached out his head to it and gave it a tentative lick. The last of Indalesh's fear evaporated. This was not just a wild beast. This was a wonderful being. It could *love*. How could they all have been so afraid of *this*?
She stepped close and stroked its fur. Confident now, she put her arm round Thumpus' neck and turned to the others.

'It's safe,' she called, simply. 'He's OK!' Nothing could hold Tesh and Tash back. Like arrows from a bow, they flew towards their friend and their grandmother, ignoring despairing calls from their parents.

'Isn't he *wonderful*!' shouted Tash, jumping round Thumpus.

<Now you must meet my mum and dad,> sent Tesh. <Names, Prush and Lelesh.>

<Not with sticks,> sent Thumpus hastily. Prush and Lelesh were advancing uncertainly through the forest towards them, gripping their sticks.

'Come and meet him. Put your sticks down,' shouted Tesh back across the woods. Prush and Lelesh hesitated. Then they laid their sticks on the woodland floor and walked closer, till they, too, felt the loving energy given off by the great animal. Tentative hands touched the fur, stroked.

Old Thumpus felt the urge to do something that only baby wumpii do with their mother. He rolled over, legs in the air, exposing his chest and belly, thick with downy, yellowy-cream fur....

The Chronicles of Thumpus Wumpus

5.
To The Village

<Thumpus, my Gorgeous One,> sent Tesh, as the children cuddled the basking animal in the place where they had first met, the 'gurgli glade, as they had come to call it, <It's time to introduce you to the village.>

In the days since the conversion of their parents and gran, Tash and Tesh, freer than ever before to be in the forest, had spent all their spare time with their 'Thumping One'. They neglected their friends, their lessons and their various duties in the euphoria of being with the telepathic beast. People were getting suspicious and all sorts of rumours were flying round.

Tesh and Thumpus were becoming more and more in tune. She could 'hear' him at home in bed now, and he could hear her, however widely he ranged in the forest. Tash was a little jealous, but even he was beginning to get impressions which might, or might not convey Thumpus' thoughts. The house stank, to Lelesh's dismay, but the children were quite accustomed to the distinctive Thumpus odour.

At Tesh's thought, Thumpus came out of the indolent reverie which he felt was his true nature, and wuffled lightly. More problems, just when things are good!

<Don't want to!>

'Don't want what,' said Tash, half picking up the thought.

'He doesn't want to meet the people,' replied Tesh. <You're just a lazy, sloppy old poot!> she continued affectionately, turning to Thumpus. 'All you like to do is lie with your legs in the air and get cuddled.' She scrambled up on to the great beast's chest and scratched through the thick fur with her bent fingers.

<Oh, bliss,> sent Thumpus, unequivocally accepting the insult. Tesh slid down.

<We are going to prepare the way,> she told Thumpus, grandly. Tash left his position cuddling Thumpus' neck and came to hold Tesh's hand.

'Laziness is not a virtue, even in thumps,' he toned sanctimoniously, remembering moral dressing downs at home. 'And I bet you are the laziest thumpus wumpus that ever lived!' Tesh translated.

<This is how wumpii should be,> sent Thumpus, defensively, <me, old wumpus - deserve peace.>

<Nonsense. You aren't old at all. World full of new things and village is next one to discover!>

Thumpus only wuffled once more and with fond goodbyes the children strode purposefully from the glade. Now they knew the way back, it seemed impossible that they could ever have been lost there. The kitchen at home was hung full of magnificent gurgli being dryed for the winter. There would be a bottling evening very soon, as well.

Left alone, Thumpus cursed his fate. Where was all this going to lead, he thought, ruefully.

'We'll never talk them round,' said Tash, as the family gathered to discuss.

'That's for sure,' agreed Prush. 'What should we do? Rumours are going all round the village already. Some are talking of a hunting party - Thumpus has been so noisy since he met us all - so near, as well.'

'Talk's talk,' said Indalesh, 'but what your own eyes see is another matter altogether. If we all came into the village with Thumpus; if he sat down with us outside your house, if they saw us all petting him - that would do the trick. But would he do it, Tesh?'

Tesh, able to communicate directly with Thumpus, was the expert.

'He would hate it at first. But as soon as everybody liked him and petted him he'd be over the moon. He still thinks people want to kill him to eat. He can't believe that anyone's really afraid of him, even now. So the hardest part for him is experiencing their fear.'

Now Tash had an idea.

'Tell him that humans are afraid of anything new and different; that it's not about him *personally,* then he won't be so upset.'

'Could we give him a wash first,' said Lelesh, 'so he doesn't look so wild and stink so!' She wrinkled her nose. The ineradicable, ever present odour of Thumpus was always around the house now.

'No chance.' Tesh was firm. 'At this stage, that would drive him away. We'll have to get him used to that really slowly.' She grinned broadly at the thought of scrubbing and grooming the protesting Thumpus. Luckily Thumpus himself was far away, trying to get at the honey in a wild bees' nest without getting dreadfully stung, and did not notice her thought.

They made a plan. Tesh and Tash would persuade and prepare Thumpus. Then they'd all meet just inside the woods, on a Sunday, after lunch, when everyone was around the village. They would walk ostentatiously, with Thumpus, to their house, where he would lie down and be stroked and cuddled. The other children would not be able to resist this, and their parents would have to come, too. As soon as they were close to him, everyone would fall under his spell.

When they sneaked off into the woods to meet Thumpus later that day, Tash was quite shocked by the way Tesh played the politician. Thumpus was in a good mood, being full of honey, and virtually stingless. A sting or two didn't bother him much, as long as there weren't too many. He had imaged *such* a glorious glade, full of wild flowers, and only a short distance away, that almost every bee who could fly had left the next to find it. By the time they came back, deceived and frustrated, to find their nest despoiled, Thumpus was well away through the forest. He licked remnants of honey from his whiskers.

<You see,> sent Tesh as persuasively as she could, elaborating their plan, <they're all *dying* to meet you. It's just that humans are really scared of anything new. Whoever wants to get over that fear has to be quite brave. It's not about you, personally. It would be the same with anyone at all. So we worked out a plan.>

<No way,> sent back Thumpus, amiably. <Not going into village for - for all honey in woods.> The thought of so much honey was most delicious. He lay back to be stroked. He particularly liked the way Tash fondled his neck.

<But they'll like you *so* much,> Tesh went on. <Problem is, we've got lots of work to do in the day time. This way you'll be able to come and visit us at home in the evening. Other people will want to cuddle you, too. You can't deny others all that pleasure. It's your *duty* to come Thumpus.>

<Don't have duty. Do as I please.> The indolent brute relaxed even more. A great belch burst from him. He had overeaten. But the thought of being liked by all those people was enticing. He wondered what the 'houses' were like inside.

Tesh winked at Tash. She had picked up the thought.

<Fascinating,> she sent. <Some even have bees' nests in eaves.>Part of Thumpus knew he was being manipulated. But he was well fed, lazy and careless.

<Be honey, then?>

Tesh thought quickly. One of the villagers, Suresh, kept hives. Honey was a precious and strictly rationed commodity in the village. But Tesh would get some somehow.

<Of course, plenty!>

<Come, Sunday?> Tash was practising thought sending. Being around Thumpus seemed to stimulate something in his brain. He had picked up Thumpus' receptive mood, and even something of his thoughts. Thumpus turned his great, warm, affectionate, brown eyes on the boy.

<You, now?> he sent, pleased. Tesh pounced on the thought.

<Everyone'll learn if you come.> She pictured the villagers all gathering around Thumpus, showing him their admiration.

<Never lonely inside me?>

'Poor Thumpus, how you must have suffered,' thought Tesh.

<Never lonely!> sent both of the children. Thumpus was finally convinced.

<Alright,> he sent. <Sunday. Now scratch tummy, please.> Tash and Tesh willingly obliged.

After an early shower, Sunday cleared up well. The plan was for Tesh and Tash to meet Thumpus and bring him to the edge of the forest, where they would meet Prush, Lelesh and Indalesh. All of them would stroll in a leisurely way to the village centre and the children's house, where Thumpus would lie down and be stroked. After Sunday lunch everyone would be well fed and relaxed. The little hamlet was alive with rumours, especially among the other children. Tash and Tesh had been unable to resist spreading the news that something special would happen that Sunday.

<You ready, Thumpus,> sent Tesh as they entered the woods. Everyone was nervous. Would the people be too scared to see that Thumpus was harmless and loveable.

<Uneasy,> returned Thumpus. <Not good idea. Give up.>

<Thumpus, you agreed. No going back now.>

<How about tomorrow?>

<Tomorrow'll be just the same,> sent both the children, approaching the spot where he was lying, tail twitching slightly, enough to make little booming wumps on the ground. <Today's the day.> Tash and Tesh reached the nervous animal, tickling his neck to soothe him.

<Up you get, now! Prush, Lelesh and Indalesh waiting.> Thumpus sighed and slowly, raising himself to his full height, stretched. He would not be hurried.The others were standing just inside the trees. Their nervousness was greater than the childrens' and worried Thumpus a lot.

<If everything all right, why nerves?> he sent urgently to Tesh.

<Oh, just humans, always nervous at any new thing.> She tried to seem confident. Indalesh stepped forward, sensing the problem and, reaching up, put her arm round Thumpus' neck. At her gesture of affection, he was somewhat reassured.

<Now remember,> sent Tesh, <there'll be lots of fear at first, but stick it out. When they see we love you and aren't afraid of you, they'll start getting curious.> Thumpus wuffled. Why had he got himself into this?

They left the trees and began to walk across the cleared land towards the houses. Almost immediately a shout went up. One of the other children had sneaked behind them.

'Help, Oh, Help! A Beast! A terrible beast from the forest! It's coming!' the child shrieked in a high pitched voice, running off towards the village. Tash saw that it was Cush, a boy a year or two younger than them.

'Lord save us,' said Lelesh, half under her breath, 'now they'll all know, before we reach the house.'

Men and women began appearing from houses, grabbing at staves leaning outside the doors. The other children peered from behind them. Before Thumpus and the others reached the village they were faced by almost everyone else, giving forth such a strong aura of fear that Thumpus was terrified.

<Run, run!> he sent, loudly, adding to the fear all around. He half turned. It was Tash, Tesh and Indalesh who saved the situation.

<Don't be afraid yourself,> sent Tesh. <Remember, only like this at first. Then good.> Tash clung to the huge beast's shoulder.

<Love you,> he sent simply. Indalesh stepped forward and addressed the little crowd in front of them.

'This is Thumpus Wumpus,' she said, loudly and decisively. 'We have tamed him. He is friendly and wants to meet you. Don't be afraid!'

It was Suresh, the beekeeper, who shouted back.

'How do we know? Maybe it's just a trick so it can get in amongst us? Don't trust it! Come away, quick.' Others nodded and gripped their staves more tightly.

Thumpus was sweating. His shaggy fur was all clammy.

<Lie down,> sent Tesh. <Quickly - on your back. As we planned at the house. We'll cuddle you.> All Thumpus' instincts howled, 'Run away! Run away!' But he looked for a moment into the eyes of the girl he had befriended and slowly, with a wump of his tail that boomed over the clearing and sent the watching people reeling back, he lay down and put his legs in the air. 'Maybe I'll die now,' he thought, defenceless, open to jabs of staves.

The little crowd gasped. Deliberately Tash clambered onto the massive chest and, clutching Thumpus' fur with one hand, waved the other.

'Look, he's *wonderful*! Jashe, Potish, Rinesh - come and see! You can stroke him!'

The scene was extraordinary - a huge wild animal, on his back, exposing his vulnerable belly, with a small boy sitting on top of him. Tesh, fondling his neck, tears in her eyes for love of Thumpus and his bravery. Prush and Lelesh, like a guard of honour, one on each side, each gently holding an upraised leg and Indalesh at the beast's head, beckoning with all the authority of her age and experience.

It was dark-haired Jashe, a good friend of Tash and Tesh, who broke the deadlock. She had been wondering for some days why her friends were so evasive, wanting to be by themselves all the time. This was the surprise they had hinted at. She dodged round her parents and ran forward.

'He's amazing,' she shouted. 'Can I touch him, too?'

'Of course you can,' said Tash. 'That's why he's here.' Jashe stroked Thumpus' fur, which was damp.

'He's all wet.'

'He's very frightened,' explained Tesh. 'He's sweating.'

'Come!' shouted Jashe to the crowd. 'He's marvellous.' But the other children were already on their way. The grown ups, not quite releasing their hold on the staves, followed slowly. The fear in the air ebbed.

<Worst moment of whole life!> sent Thumpus to Tesh and Tash. But he knew it was already past. New things were going to happen. Life would change. It was going to be worth it!

The Chronicles of Thumpus Wumpus

6.
Entry and breaking

As Thumpus made his way towards the little collection of log houses, surrounded by still-cautious villagers, his fear abated. The enormous anxiety to which he had responded had ebbed; now an intense curiosity replaced it. It was difficult not to feel proud to be the object of so much attention after the years of isolation he had endured. But the sight of a couple of children holding their noses deflated him somewhat. Finicky little beasts!

<Good smell,> he sent, a little aggressively. All around people picked up the thought, without knowing its origin.

'Awful smell,' they thought to themselves, shaking their heads. Thumpus was taken aback. Was human company going to be as pleasurable as he anticipated? There seemed to be such a lot of ready judgement around. Only Tesh and Tash, who were used to the odour, responded differently.

'Bearable smell,' they thought. 'Other qualities make up for it.' Poor Thumpus almost felt worse. His trusted friends had to put up with him. Where was the unconditional love he expected? Anyway, he didn't smell at all. It was *they* who smelled. And it was *dreadful* - all carbolic and turpentine. Not natural at all. Thumpus began to sulk, but the mood didn't last more than a moment because now they were entering the village itself. 'Wooden caves,' he thought. 'Not bad with snow coming. Keep a Thumpus warm and dry. Lots of different smells - food!'

They arrived at Tash and Tesh's house, much like the others, made of rough logs with a good turf roof.

'Welcome,' cried Tash and Tesh together excitedly. 'This is our house.'

A more diffident welcome came from Prush and Lelesh.

'What on earth are we going to do with him?' they whispered to each other. Thumpus picked up the thought, but he was by now surrounded by delighted children, petting him, scrambling over him and overcoming their resistance to the strange odour that was going to pervade the village from now on. Thumpus decided that young humans were the nicest of all. It was through them he was here. He felt like giving a really loud wump, but realised that a good swing of his thumpus might hit the children swarming around him, so held back with an effort. Even some of the adults were plucking up courage to approach and gingerly stroke his scruffy fur. Smell or no, he really was irresistible.

Tesh spoke with Suresh.

'All my saved-up pocket money for a big jar of honey?'

'*And* two days' work in my garden for you *and* your brother,' returned Suresh.

Tesh groaned. 'All right,' she conceded. It was so important that Thumpus got off to a good start. They left the crowd around Thumpus and crossed to Suresh's house. Suresh had no partner and was considered a little mean, but he had a monopoly on honey production in the village, the only one who knew the secrets of how to manage bees. In a moment they returned to the centre of attention, carrying a large jar.

'I want that back,' said Suresh pointedly. 'It's not part of the deal.' Big glass jars were precious. They had to be imported to the village and it took a great deal of honey to pay for one. Tesh nodded and marched proudly to Thumpus, who was engaging the crowd around him with his big, doleful brown eyes.

<Here's what I promised,> she sent proudly. And, aside, to Tash, 'Two days' work. You've got to help.' Tash groaned in his turn.

<Bit like honey,> sent Thumpus, as he regarded the jar. <Smells like honey. Very like honey,> he added, as Tesh wrestled to undo the jar.

<*Is* honey!> he communicated in a sort of soft moan as the lid came off and the penetrating smell overwhelmed him.

<Just for you,> sent Tesh simply, as she placed the jar in front of the drooling animal. - the sound was cut off as Thumpus' snout entered the jar. Big as it was, it was too small for him to get his head into as he would have liked. Honey was a rare delicacy for Thumpus, in spite of his recently found nest, and this honey seemed to be without the retribution of bee stings. The jar was a nuisance, though. As he pushed eagerly in at it, the honey seemed to swell up, pouring all over his face. It was so sticky, he could hardly open his jaws to let his tongue get at it. But he managed!

In no time at all, the only honey left was all over Thumpus' muzzle. An overwhelming urge came upon him.

<Back!> he sent demandingly. The children who were on his back picked up the thought and fell off, rushing to their parents, who also retreated hastily. Thumpus' tail swung in an enormous circle, almost touching the cowering crowd and crashed into the ground with a hollow boom that echoed over the village and into the forest beyond. Gasps came from the onlookers.

'That's what we've been afraid of all these years!' It was Indalesh who spoke first. 'But it's because he's happy that he does it.' Thumpus looked slowly round the little group, who were beginning to recover from the shock. If he could have grinned, he would certainly have done so. As it was, he managed a sort of lopsided leer, and a glint entered those big brown eyes.

<Not bad one!> he sent, at peace with the world.

After a while, the moment Lelesh had been fearing arrived.

<Come into our house,> invited Tash and Tesh. <It's a good house. You'll like it. But no thumps inside, please. You'd break everything.> Thumpus eyed the doorway.

<Small,> he sent. <Too small. Why such little hole?>

<You'll make it,> sent Tesh. <Bigger inside.>

'Wait!' cried Lelesh urgently. She thought of all the little things she had put up to make the place homely and comfortable. Of the bunches of gurgli hanging to dry above the stove. Of clean washing drying from the rack before it. But she knew that she couldn't forbid Thumpus' entry. It had all been building up to this.

'Wait,' she said again, more calmly. 'Give me five minutes, while I arrange things.' She pushed the door open and ran inside. Hastily, breakable things were pushed through the inner door. 'Whatever they want, he's not going into the bedrooms,' she thought determinedly. Still, it was exciting that Thumpus would come in. Such a strange and attractive animal.

'All right,' she called out, the most fragile objects more or less out of the way, 'he can come in now - if he can get in.'

Thumpus' head and shoulders emerged through the opening. If he stood straight, his shoulders nearly touched the top of the door and brushed the sides. Tesh was right. He could make out the darker room, lit by a hole at the side; the door was the smallest bit. He pushed through and took a step or two across the rough stone floor. His tail was not yet inside. He took another step and began to turn to look around. It was a good den, warm and comfortable. A bit too warm! As he turned his tail knocked over a chair and made for the hot stove.

'Stop!' yelled Tash, Tesh and Prush, who had followed him in. 'Stop!' yelled Lelesh from the other side of the room. Thumpus froze.

<Hot. Burn tail!> Tesh sent a horrible image of a smoking, blackened tail. Thumpus shivered. He felt an an-

guished, pain-releasing wump coming on, but controlled it with an effort. Tesh and Tash were at his neck, consoling him. Disentangling himself very carefully, keeping his tail from the mysterious and deadly stove, he moved forward to the far corner of the room, near Lelesh, lifted his tail gingerly and began to turn. A large earthenware pot that Lelesh had thought well out of the way up on a shelf, crashed to the floor and broke.

'My best stew pot!' she cried out despairingly. This was worse than she had feared. She should have known that Thumpus was just too large to come in. Besides, the smell was overpowering.

'It's no use,' said Prush, firmly, voicing all their thoughts, even those of Thumpus, 'he's too big.' He did not want to hurt their new friend's feelings, and bottled up the 'and too clumsy' that wanted to follow, but Thumpus picked up the feeling all the same. He wuffled softly and everything shook. People outside craned their heads into the room. Fear was rising again. Was the beast not to be trusted after all? Prush had an inspiration.

'I'll build him a house outside,' he said triumphantly. 'You two can help,' he said to Tash and Tesh. 'He's your beast, really.'

<Me my own beast,> thought Thumpus. But he understood. The place was just too small with all the clutter of things in it. He carefully turned to the door, knocking over another chair, and pushed his way back out, as the group looking in made way.

<Own house,> he thought, pleased. Everyone had the same idea and nodded. A solution had been found.

Thumpus triumphantly toured the little village - outside the houses - led by Tash and the other children. Everyone was warming to him, even surly old Suresh, whose heart was melted somewhat by Thumpus' relish of his honey. Anyone who liked honey that much must be OK really. But Indalesh,

Lelesh and half a dozen of the other women were meeting together. Tesh, now expert and chief communicator with their new-found friend was also present.

'He'll have to be washed. There's no alternative. I'm not having my children bringing home that stink day after day.' Alesh, mother of Jashe and Potish, was firm and clear. Heads nodded agreement on all sides. Only Tesh was hesitant. While she basically agreed with the others, she was afraid of Thumpus' response.

'He thinks he's fine as he is,' she protested. He might run away if we try to clean him up.'

'He won't,' said Indalesh. 'He's much too happy to be here. I'm sure he'll grumble, but if we all take part and comb and groom him afterwards, he'll accept it.' Tesh was not so sure, but had to accept that it was very unlikely that Thumpus would run away. His happy feelings were all around her, even here. And every now and again, joyful wumps resounded through the village. The children egged him on to do them again and again.

Lelesh formulated the plan. 'We'll each bring a bucket of warm soapy water and scrubbing brushes. He'll probably like to be brushed dry with them. When the time is right, we'll dip them in the water and then you'll have to keep him calm, Tesh. Get all the other children to help. Finally, we'll see if he can be persuaded to rinse off in the stream. He'll probably be happy to do it, to get rid of the soap.'

It seemed simple enough. They would wait till the early evening, give Thumpus a good meal of cooked meat and vegetables so he was replete and semi-comatose, then carry out the plan.

'He'll be cold after that,' objected Tesh lamely. 'He'll shiver all night, and his house isn't built yet. It'll take at least a week.'

Nashe, Rinesh's mother, sniffed.

'Poor thing,' she said sarcastically, 'all these years he's lived out in the rain and snow, and now you're worried about a little water. Don't turn him into a softie.' She was always very concerned that Rinesh, whom she adored, would be tough and independent. Rinesh, sensing this, tended to be insecure and clinging - to make sure she really did love him - in turn irritating Nashe. It was a difficult relationship.

The plan, was finally agreed upon and everyone else informed. Thumpus was still gambolling around the village with the delighted children. Normally, his acute inner sense would have picked up the scheming. It was the only real defensive system Thumpus Wumpii had, and they rarely let it down. Otherwise, they perished. But all the new feelings and excitements overwhelmed Thumpus. He was vulnerable.

In addition to the family meal, Prush and Lelesh cooked a couple of rabbits in the second-largest stew pot. Others cooked potatoes and carrots. The whole was flavoured with salt, rosemary and marjoram. Before anyone else ate, the treat was presented to the village's pet, who had returned to the house of Tesh and Tash, his favourites. He lay outside, lolling around, enjoying the smells wafting from the cottage door. Tesh had told him that some would be for him!

The others arrived with steaming pots of tatties and carrots. The succulent rabbits, perfectly stewed, were brought out.

'Bliss,' he thought, as he began to tuck in to the pile of food tipped before him on the biggest earthenware dish the village possessed. 'This is how a Thumpus Wumpus *should* live.' He was hungry after the experiences of the day and ignored other, less pleasant thoughts that seemed to be lurking around. The meal tasted delicious. Absolutely exquisite. Just enough for a starving animal. The last crumbs consumed, Thumpus lay back and relaxed, watching the sun dipping away to the west.

'Oh pleasant, pleasant afternoon. Oh happy, happy Thumpus,' he thought. His tummy rumbled. He belched contentedly.

The cleaning party assembled quietly. Sleepily, Thumpus acknowledged them. All the children, who had been informed of the plan, gathered at his head.

<We'd like to brush you,> sent Tesh. <It's even nicer than being stroked.>

<Try,> returned the replete beast, totally off-guard. The ensuing rubbing of the brushes along his fur felt good, very good.

<Harder,> urged the hapless animal, sending images of firm hands pushing brushes deep into his coat. The children pulled out twigs, releasing tangles.

'What Thumpus ever experienced such bliss before?' wondered Thumpus in a self-satisfied way, rolling onto his back.

When the worst of the tangles were out, Lelesh gave the signal. Calmly turning, as if nothing was happening at all, six pairs of hands reached for six large buckets, full of warm, soapy water. The buckets were tipped, and dear, smelly Thumpus was flooded from head to tail with sticky wetness. The scrubbing instantly began anew, bringing the wetness from outside to inside the fur, warm soap dissolving the oils brought out by the grooming.

<Lovely warm water, cleaning, good smell,> sent Tesh as convincingly as she could (she was not over-fond of washing herself). Tash, not so skilled, did his best to send the same thoughts.

Thumpus was so relaxed, so off-guard, that it took several moments for the horrible reality to penetrate.

<Traitors! Betrayed!> he sent in a wail, and, with a convulsive shudder, scattering washers and children to all sides, leapt up and raced for the forest, shaking himself and soaking everyone in the vicinity as he did so.

<Oh misery! Oh horror! Oh cruelty! Oh betrayal!> Thumpus' anguished emotions hit the village like a tidal wave. People sat and held their heads. Tesh and Tash, closest of all physically and mentally, were devastated. Crying, they began to run after the stricken animal.

Thumpus ran for the river. He had to get the ghastly stinking stickiness off. He leapt the 2-metre fence of the goat pen, sending the startled beasts in all directions, and threw himself in their drinking pool, where the river ran through the pen.

<Death! Horrors! Betrayal!> The thoughts still surrounded him as he wallowed, rolling on his back in the muddy water. Shivering - from nerves rather than cold - he twisted and turned in the dirty mud at the edge of the pool, and then, leaping the fence again, was away, into the woods, running as if he would never stop through the trees towards the westering sun.

Tash and Tesh, tears streaming from their faces, followed closely by the other children, ran up to the goat pen, just in time to see a huge, muddy, dripping form disappearing into the forest. In a second, he was gone.

'No, no, no!' they cried as their new-found happiness dissolved in the fading sunlight.

<Come back, come back! We love you,> sent Tesh despairingly, with all her might at the place where Thumpus had dissolved into the trees. There was no reply.

The Chronicles of Thumpus Wumpus

7.
Kamal

The whole village was devastated. Their special new friend had run away. The event was discussed endlessly and all agreed it had been a mistake to try to trick Thumpus. No-one had expected such an intense reaction. After all, they were only trying to clean him up, to get rid of a fraction of the pong he carried around him.

Two days passed with no sign of the animal. Perhaps occasional wumps could be heard, but so faint and far away that no-one could be sure. Tash and Tesh, who had first found and befriended Thumpus, became depressed and withdrawn. They wouldn't eat properly. They wouldn't work. They wouldn't learn. When Suresh came around seeking work as re-payment for his honey, Lelesh had to send him away fuming.

'You'll have to go and try to find him,' said Indalesh eventually. She was angry with herself for not being sensitive enough to foresee Thumpus' reaction and veto the plan. 'The children are pining away.'

Reluctantly, Lelesh and Prush agreed. The rest of the villagers did not dispute the idea. The two best hunters, Minesh and Tansh, said they would accompany the others.

Next morning, a little group, consisting of Lelesh, Prush, Minesh, Tansh, Tash and Tesh, knapsacks slung on their shoulders, adults carrying sharpened staves for protection, set out from the village to cross the forest to the west, the direction Thumpus had disappeared.

It had been very difficult for Prush and Lelesh to agree to bring Tesh and Tash. They were going into unknown territory, with the possibility of getting lost. Although reassured that Thumps were not dangerous and knowing from Thumpus that there were not many of them anyway, they feared there might be other, unknown terrors. Sharpened sticks were their only means of defence. Nobody paid much attention to weapons in the village. If you don't fight, who needs weapons?

On the other hand, Tesh and Tash had been adamant that they must go. They had discovered Thumpus and were his primary friends. They had shared in the plan - now acknowledged as a total disaster - to wash the smelly beast, and were devastated at his abrupt departure. Travelling would get them out of their depression. Above all, it was Tesh who could communicate with Thumpus across considerable distances. If they were to have any chance of finding him and making up, she was the key. It was this argument that finally convinced Prush and Lelesh. And of course, if you took Tesh, Tash had to come, too.

The little group made their way through the woods in a westerly direction, orienting by the sun, which shone brightly. They avoided thick underbrush, and forded streams. Luckily, it had not rained much recently. The villagers were not great explorers and were inexperienced in the kind of country they traversed.

However, at first the hunters had some idea of the land around them. Although they did not make fast progress, they were hardy and fit and travelled steadily. By nightfall they had gone some 25 kilometres across the hills, the limit of the hunters' knowledge. They camped, building a fire, ate some food and settled down for the night, wriggling into their 'snugs', as everyone called their goat-hair sleeping bags. The hunters and Prush and Lelesh arranged to share a watch between them.

Tesh lay long awake, sending despairing thoughts and apologies to Thumpus, but there was no reply. As the morning sunlight flooded the cool forest, all were asleep.

Thumpus ran and ran. He had never run so fast or so far in one go. He moved towards the west, to the setting sun and, as the dusk gathered, he continued to run, but more carefully, veering a little north and using all his senses to avoid trees and roots. Finally, panting heavily, he stopped. He was dangerously close to the territory of Kamal, the cantankerous old bear, but he didn't care. The world was an awful place now and if he was eaten up, so what! His head ached, he was hungry, and his heart felt as if someone had tried to rip it out of his chest.

Love! He had given love, the first time he had had the chance since his cubhood long ago, and he had been betrayed. So quickly! They just wanted to turn him into their creature, make him a little pet, smelling of pine soap and yuck. He might not be much, but he was a Thumpus and he had a sense of his own identity! Thoughts turned and turned in Thumpus' brain in an endless circling. At least he was free of that ghastly village and those terrible children who had betrayed him. He would never, *never* see any of them *ever* again. He would live in another part of the forest, alone, *alone*. Misery consumed him and he yowled in pain like a starter violinist. Kamal heard, was afraid and miserable too, and kept well away from the area.

In the morning it was worse, if anything. Conflicting thoughts plagued him now - Perhaps they didn't have bad intentions - they just didn't understand Thumpii. If he hadn't run away, perhaps he could have explained to them that Thumpus-smell is just part of a Thumpus, like skin. He didn't mind them brushing his fur, after all. Perhaps Tesh - Tesh's taking part in the washing hurt the most - had been made to do it against her will, though he hadn't picked up any such thoughts from her. If he hadn't been so lazy and distracted, perhaps he could have thought them out of the idea.

He rejected all these 'perhapses', but they wouldn't go away. Now he began to miss Tash and Tesh, Indalesh, Prush and Lelesh and even the new friends he had met. Friends!

So his misery continued, alternating between resentment, loneliness, loss and self-doubt. He absently nibbled at some plants, which gave him tummy ache. He remembered the honey at the village. Tesh had said there would be lots of it! So the miserable day passed and another wretched night.

Next morning he began to feel he shouldn't have run away at all. Perhaps he was just a proud old Thumpus. He had run away from a life richer than any he had ever known, from someone who he could talk with inside and from others who might learn. What a miserable beast he was! Everything mixed in a jumble in his head, till he hardly knew what he was doing. He spent several hours going round and round following his tail, till he was giddy and exhausted. Every living thing had been frightened away by his awful mood. He managed to find a few grubs in a rotting piece of wood, but he was getting dreadfully hungry. Luckily, Kamal, outside the range of the moods Thumpus was broadcasting, had managed to catch a deer, and was enjoying his full stomach. Thumpus passed yet another dreadful night. He was making himself ill.

The morning after that, Thumpus knew he would have to go back if he wasn't to die of misery in the forest. All his pride rebelled, but there was no alternative. As a compromise, he decided to wait till the next day. 'Perhaps they're missing me as much as I miss them,' he thought resentfully. The decision made things a little better. He drank deeply from a nearby stream and found some tasty wild parsnip roots in a clearing! In the morning he would go back!

He slept much better, waking up to enjoy the slip of a hazy moon through the canopy of trees. He even managed a very modest wump.

The search party set out again, into unknown territory. They were themselves now having doubts. It was a wild goose chase, or rather, a wild and wilful Thumpus chase! They could get lost very easily. Hopefully, they would be able to follow a stream downwards and eventually come out of the woods somewhere, but would their food hold out? Tesh, however, felt better.

'I'm sure he's thinking about us,' she confided to Tash, whose mood had also lifted. He was beginning to enjoy the adventure. Still, Tesh could not detect any clear indication that Thumpus was around and, as the morning wore on and they tramped further and further through the woods, she began to feel a vague foreboding, a sense that they were walking into danger. She didn't say anything at first. She knew that the adults were already worried.

They stopped in a clearing for lunch. It was pleasant enough and the stream water tasted good. But the sky was becoming greyer and there was a cold feel in the air. Minesh glanced at Tansh.

'Snow in the offing.' Tansh just nodded. It was the most dangerous thing. They could hole up all right in a real blizzard - there was plenty of fallen wood to make a rough shelter - but if it lay deep they could neither find their way, nor move any distance.

'Might turn to rain,' Minesh continued doubtfully. He was thinking the same thoughts as Tansh. More likely, a sign of the first real winter storm.

The little party sat disconsolately in the clearing, chewing at cheese sandwiches with pickles. No-one spoke much. Tesh's foreboding mounted.

Kamal, the giant bear, padded through the woods. It was going to snow. Lucky he'd killed that deer. He licked his lips. Soon it would be time to hole up in his cave and let the winter cold pass him by. In spring he'd go hunting a mate, high up in the mountains. He stopped. Bad smells! Something was in his territory. Angrily he curled his lip back from his ferocious teeth and gave a soft growl. He padded off in the direction of the scent.

It was almost a new smell, but not quite. There had been one like it before, from a nasty thing with a sharp pointed stick that pricked before he smashed it with his paw. From the smell, he could tell there was more than one this time. Cautiously, he approached the clearing which he now located as the source of the scent. It was right in the middle of his territory, *his* bit of the woods. He snarled silently once more.

'There's something coming this way!' Tesh said suddenly. 'It's not Thumpus. It's angry and violent.'

Everyone jumped up, grabbed their sticks and began peering into the woods surrounding the clearing in the direction Tesh indicated. Prush saw it first - a huge, malevolent shadow in the trees, that instantly became an enormous bear which identified itself with a bloodcurdling roar.

'We'll never keep that off!' Tansh's teeth were set. 'Up trees! High! Fast!'

Kamal hesitated, regarding them angrily. He could see four with prickers and two little ones. Luckily for the group, he was not hungry or he wouldn't have paused. He began to move forward, snarling. The little ones ran for the edge of the clearing and jumped into trees. The prickers gave ground more slowly. At a shout, they, too, turned and ran for trees. Kamal was in no hurry. There was snow on the way. It would freeze them out of the tree tops. He could wait. He raised himself up against the nearest occupied tree and dragged his great claws down it, smashing the small branches the humans had used to climb up and leaving deep claw marks in the bark. Kamal would wait. The first, tentative snowflake drifted down from a leaden sky. Both Kamal and the hunters knew that the wait would not be too long.

Huddled with Tash high up in a tree, Tesh shivered. The big old pine hadn't been difficult to climb, though some of the dead branches below had hardly borne their weight. The great beast had smashed many of them with its claws. The atmosphere was full of fear and anger, blind, insentient rage. Controlling her fear, she sent, with all her energy, a thought:

<Help! Trapped! Huge, angry beast! Come quickly!>

A few kilometres away to the north, Thumpus was just setting out on his way back to the village. He had dithered and hesitated, still caught between hurt dignity and his sense of loss, but the knowledge of the impending snowfall decided him. Even if they hadn't built him a hut yet, he could make himself go to Tesh and Tash's house again, if he was *very* careful. He thought of Tesh and Tash cuddling him and began to move purposefully back through the woods.

Tesh's thought was far away, from nowhere near the village, which was a long way to the south east. It came from direct south. Right from Kamal's territory. How could they be there? The sense came again, just on the edge of awareness:

<Help! Angry beast! Come!>

Thumpus began to run through the trees and underbrush as fast as he could, towards the south.

In an hour, he could sense the thoughts more easily, even though they were sent with less power. He also began to feel the patient anger of the great bear and the general fear. Snowflakes twisted lazily through the trees. He was hot from running, but he knew it was becoming colder.

<Thumpus coming! Climb tree!> he sent urgently. Nothing could resist Kamal's onslaught if he was really furious and, from the atmosphere Thumpus could detect, he seemed to be.

<In trees already. There's a terrible, angry, huge animal. Six of us. We're very cold. Please help!> Tesh's thought

was clear now. Another <Help!> came through as well - Tash was sending.

'Good lad - he's learning,' went through Thumpus' mind. Now he must be clever. The wind was from the north, behind him. If he went any closer, Kamal would scent him. Kamal had a very good sense of smell He'd have to go round and approach from the side. He could get much closer that way, but it'd take more time. From the east, away from Kamal's lair.

<Wait! Coming!> sent Thumpus and moved off through the woods.

'Thumpus is coming!' shouted Tesh to the others in the nearby treetops. Below them, Kamal roared at the noise and barged at the tree, shaking even its sturdy girth. Tash and Tesh grabbed at their branches. For Tansh and Minesh the news seemed no great consolation. They had only just met Thumpus, a pleasant, hairy thing, all cuddles and good nature. The others knew that Thumpus could also be resourceful and cunning and was a master telepath. In spite of the cold, their spirits lifted. The snowflakes drifted down, a little thicker.

Thumpus, now knowing his friends had come for him just as he was on his way to them, ran fast to circle round the clearing where Kamal had treed them. Indeed, he realised, they must have set out while he, Thumpus, was being a misery. They *must* love him really! He felt a moment of shame, but then resumed his total concentration on moving through the terrain as fast as possible.

To him, it was not long before, panting with heat, he arrived in a position just out of sight of the clearing. To the others, still and shivering in the trees, it seemed hours. Their packs, with extra warm things, were by the now dead fire. Kamal had left them alone. To him, fire was the worst enemy.

<How get him away?> Thumpus' thought was loud in Tesh's head. He was behind them in the trees, close now. <Him obstinate, vicious beast.>

<Pretend you're very big and fierce - make him run away.> Tesh could not help a grin at the thought. Thumpus was big all right, but this thing was twice his size, at least.

<Just make him fight. His territory.> Thumpus' cunning mind was at work. <Him lonely. Pretend female arrived, behind, near den. He go see. Then - run!> Thumpus sent a clear picture to Kamal of another, smaller bear, wandering near a rock pile a kilometre away to the west. He had seen them together once and knew they had mated. After the cub had grown, female and cub had left the area.

Kamal stirred uneasily. There seemed to be a wonderful, miraculous scent coming from his lair. Surely Kemba couldn't have returned. Not after all this time! It had been years. If so, they could spend the cold winter together in the lair.

<Send it, too,> Thumpus urged Tesh, trying to reinforce the image. There was even a smell to it. Tesh mimicked as best she could, though she couldn't manage the smell - she'd have to ask Thumpus about that another time.

'Thumpus is sending a picture of another bear, over there,' said Tash softly, pointing. He could definitely sense an image of a bear, off to the west, but it was blurry.

'Send it, too,' returned Tesh tersely. She was concentrating had on replicating Thumpus' image.

It was impossible, thought Kamal, but it must be true. Kemba had returned. He could picture her clearly, near the lair. Her scent was irresistible. She must have come back for him. How wonderful! Kamal would have to leave these stupid prickers this time. He got up, stretched, gave a final threatening roar at the intruders, and padded away across the clearing at an increasing speed. The snowflakes were dropping quite thickly now.

<Keep sending image,> sent Thumpus in a very fast thought. <Then get down. And away!>

'We must get down and off back to the village,' shouted Tesh, as Thumpus suddenly appeared below them. 'Follow Thumpus!'

'Dear old Thumpus!' Tash's eyes were filled with tears of joy and love. He forgot instantly about sending an image of the female bear to Kamal, but Thumpus and Tesh didn't. If Kamal returned they would have no chance, and Thumpus couldn't climb trees.

They scrambled down, crashing and dropping the last gap where Kamal's claws had torn the branches, grabbed their packs and ran after Thumpus, who set off at a cracking pace through the trees.

'Too fast! Can't keep this up for long.' Minesh was aware of the distance to the village.

But Thumpus maintained his pace. Kamal moved fast and would be at his lair soon. Kemba wouldn't be there! He'd be furious! Would he return after the invaders?

Kamal arrived at his den at a run. And stopped dead. Where was Kemba? She should be here. He was sweating with anticipation and the hard run. Usually he loped, which was comfortable and fast enough. Her scent was here all right - funny, he could *almost* see her. He let out a great roar. She must hear that and come.

Thumpus' keen ears heard it.

<Him back at den,> he warned. <Keep moving. Fast!>

For Kamal, the scent and sense of Kemba suddenly disappeared as if they had never been. There were only memories, stirred up in the bear's small and misty mind. Maddened by the loss, he howled and howled again, turning furiously around and around. The memory of the prickers in the trees returned and he pawed at the earth in rage. They would be down and gone. He made no connection between the images of Kemba and the prickers. Growling continuously, he went to where he had killed the deer. Foxes had been at the remains of the carcass, but there were still bones. In his anger and frustration, he chewed and crunched till his teeth ached. Then he returned to his lair. The snow was falling thick and fast. Lair was the best place with this weather setting in. He snuggled in a corner of it, alone, but at least comfortable. Time for sleep.

The Chronicles of Thumpus Wumpus

8.
Snow

It wasn't long before Thumpus' cracking pace was too much for the humans, but at least they were warm again. There was no sign of any pursuit. Thumpus was pretty sure that the bear would not connect the invaders of his territory with the deception. Kamal worked mainly by instinct, and a connection like that was too much for his tiny brain.

If one enemy was evaded, another - dangerous in a different way - was looming. It was snowing hard now, drifting through the trees, turning the woods into a speckled world. At present most of the snow was held off by the forest canopy, but that would change if it went on - and it looked as if it was going to go on. They were still a day out from the village and it was already late afternoon - which meant another night in the open.

Thumpus, feeling somewhat exhausted himself, marshalled the group on at a slower pace, sending to Tesh that they must be well out of Kamal's regular hunting area before they stopped. He seemed to find his way through the forest unerringly. In about another hour he led them to a deep thicket. In such weather, any animal would be glad of night shelter in a thicket this dense, and daytime creatures like humans, even more so.

Prush got a fire going with small sticks under trees so tangled that little snow had come through. Lelesh and the others began to pull fallen logs into a rough shelter. Thumpus sat and panted. He liked showing the humans that he was competent, but he was tired out after three days of emotional misery and such a lot of unwonted physical exertion. Though Tesh and Tash were also tired, they cuddled Thumpus and thought with him.

<Dear, dear old wumping, thumping, scrofulous old fuzz-buzz,> sent Tesh warmly, <how could we live without you? Why on earth did you run away like that? It was only a bit of soap and water!>

Some of Thumpus' resentment returned.

<Nasty!> he sent indignantly. <Wumpii *never* wash. Thumping Wumpii *not* humans. Live own lives in own way. Came to you *free*. Missed you very much. Was coming back,> he ended lamely.

<Oh Thumpus, we are sorry. We're all sorry. We came to find you. We wouldn't have done that if we didn't care. Village people don't often go deep into the forest.>

Thumpus knew this was true. Although he had smelled Minesh and Tansh around, hunting rabbits, he knew they were the only ones.

<Accept apology. Ask respect for new days.>

They were silent for a while, thinking about the silliness that had led to this adventure.

'If only I hadn't agreed to the washing,' thought Tesh to herself, but Thumpus heard.

'If only I hadn't run away,' thought Thumpus to himself, but Tesh heard.

'If only I could send and receive better, I could have stopped it all,' thought Tash to himself. The others received it and cuddled up to him.

Soon the adults made a very rough lean-to with fallen logs. There was plenty of moss around to fill the gaps between the logs, so a shelter, of sorts, they had. They pulled the burning fire sticks over to its entrance as soon as the kettle boiled. There was hottea for everyone. Thumpus licked snow. Tesh shared the inner conversation with the others, and Thumpus was roundly promised he'd never be washed again, though, if he wanted to do it off his own bat, nobody would stop him.

<Wumpii never wash,> was all Thumpus would return. Lelesh groaned, but when Thumpus turned his great yellowish-brown eyes on her, all sad and enquiring, she went up and cuddled him, stink or no stink. Prush felt down into the bottom of his pack and drew out a packet. Unwrapped, it was a smoked rabbit, one of their precious store for winter. He laid it on Thumpus' paws.

'Tesh, tell him I brought it in case we found him,' he said. Thumpus glowed. He had been feeling very hungry, and cheese sandwiches weren't going to be the answer. Everyone else ate cheese sandwiches.

It was now dark and snowing hard. They talked about their adventure with Kamal, clearly the legendary 'death bear' and a really dangerous beast of the forest, though Thumpus assured them he had never known Kamal to leave his territory in the west. Then there wasn't anything else to do but sleep. They all cuddled close to keep warm, except Thumpus, who wandered about a little, to make sure he knew the direction for the morning. The snow was going to be deep. In the end, nobody kept watch, but it was all right - they were sheltered from the snow storm.

Bright light - snow light. Tash opened his eyes to a white world outside their shelter. Tansh had a fire going; the others were stirring but not yet fully awake. Thumpus was nowhere to be seen. Tash shook himself from his snug cover and made for the loo place, a little away from the lean-to. The snow was deep, surely about 30 centimetres, even under the trees, but the sky was clear and frosty. Breath steamed as you let it out and bit as you drew it in. It was cold, but not *really* cold. Not like the winter cold, which froze you even in the house. Still, it was nice to go back to the little fire, where water was boiling for a hot drink. There was no wind to speak of - the smoke was going almost straight up.

They were all up, eating, and beginning to worry about Thumpus' absence when he returned, licking around his jaws with his long thick tongue. He had found a rotten tree trunk full of grubs - a tasty breakfast!

<Cold tonight,> sent Thumpus. <Village today, if can.> Tash was getting better at thought transfer. He understood, and proudly translated for the others. Tesh smiled at him and nodded. They finished eating quickly, put out the fire and set out.

It was slow walking. Thumpus broke the trail with his big, paddy feet. In the thick of the woods, the snow was shallower, but the underbrush was thicker, with snow all over it, so your trousers got soaked as you pushed through. In thinner patches, the snow was deeper, so walking was hard and your feet got icy. They went single file, to make the best use of Thumpus' hard work at the front. Minesh was rearguard, but Thumpus sent that they needn't worry about Kamal. He would have holed up in this weather. There was now nothing else in this part of the woods to hurt them.

The world around was white and black - black tree trunks standing up from white, snow-covered ground. In places, a pale blue sky showed through the branches overhead. Sometimes a sunlight sparkle would turn a little glade into fairyland. They ploughed on, trusting Thumpus to know the way. The country should have been familiar to Tansh and Minesh now, but all the ground signs they used to find the way were covered in snow.

They had lunch when the sun was highest, but it was too cold to stop for long, and they didn't spend time lighting a fire. On and on they went. Tash was very tired. It seemed much longer than the way out, and ploughing through the snow was much harder work.

Step after step - Tash counted them. His feet were like ice blocks, but he wouldn't give up. He wished they would stop and light a fire. The sky gradually turned a violet colour and darkened towards purple. It was very cold. Tash felt a little dizzy.

<Smell village smoke,> sent Thumpus. <Much worry too.>

Tash couldn't smell smoke, nor could he sense anxiety. Thumpus really was very clever indeed. The thought of how nice Thumpus was, how he was caring for them all, made him feel warm all over for a moment, keeping out the cold. Thumpus picked it up.

<Love you too. Not reach village before dark. What do?>

Tesh shared. Everyone stopped. No-one from the village would come searching for them - no-one went into the woods in the dark. You would lose your way instantly.

'Thumpus knows the way,' said Tash, reassuring the grown-ups. 'He smells the village. People there are worried about us,' he added. 'But I'm tired. Maybe we could camp?'

<Winter cold tonight,> sent Thumpus. <Camp dangerous. Not enough warmth.>

They discussed what to do. They would be totally dependent on Thumpus. But they had been anyway, ever since he'd saved them from Kamal. Everyone was feeling the cold. Thick fur wraps were needed to bear it, which they didn't have, and there was no thicket for a lean-to at this place. It would be hard to light a fire on the snow-covered ground. All agreed it was best to go on.

With the very last of the light, Minesh spied a mark she had made on a tree to find her way when out hunting.

'Two hours to the village,' she said, 'if we go fast.'

Thumpus could have gone much faster, but he was padding carefully to beat down the snow for the others. If he got ahead of them they'd probably become hopelessly lost and frightened in spite of his trail. The smell of the village and the worry centred there were quite clear to him now. Easy to go towards them. But even his paws were beginning to feel icy as the cold night began to bite. Everything was black. You had to be very close together to sense the dark form you were following in front of you.The best way was to put a hand out to feel them. Tash was definitely feeling dizzy. He began to sway from side to side. Then there was nothing.

'Stop!' yelled Prush, behind him. 'Tash has fallen!' They gathered around the boy with much anxiety. Tash was pulled from the ground. Prush felt in his pack and found a little bottle. No-one could see a thing.

'It's Rescue,' explained Prush, his gloves off in the cold, fumbling with the stopper. 'Two or three drops on the tongue should do the trick.' Somehow he managed it without dropping anything to the ground. Within seconds, Tash revived somewhat.

'We'll have to stop.' It was Lelesh. 'He'll not make it to the village.'

'Dangerous for all of us, if we stop,' said Minesh. 'You don't stay out in cold like this.'

There was a momentary, unhappy silence.

<On my back,> sent Thumpus. Tesh translated the thought to the others. There didn't seem any choice.

'Can you hold on?' Lelesh asked Tash.

'Yes.' Tash was determined not to let the party down again.

They lifted him up. He lay forward, legs down each side of Thumpus' hairy back, grabbing hold of Thumpus' fur with his hands.

'Keep your head right down - branches,' instructed Prush. They set off again. Thumpus went slowly, so as not to lose the others. He could sense their tiredness. He was tired too, but a forest animal has extra reserves. He also went slowly so as not to shake Tash off. The boy seemed pretty weak.

Tash gripped tight, head right down. There was nothing to see, but he kept his eyes open. He mustn't get dizzy again. Thumpus' muscles moved under him, and slowly warmth seeped through the animal's fur into his own body. Tash's feet were still numb, but at least there wasn't more icy snow to step in. He began to feel a little better.

On and on they went through the blackness, cold, exhausted, moving automatically. Tesh was right at the end of her strength. One leg moved before the other as if she didn't will it herself. She imagined being a female Thumpus with endless strength, coming home to the lair where her cub was waiting. Thumpus picked up the image and almost stopped, with Tansh bumping into him, before he realised it was Tesh, keeping herself going. There hadn't been a female Thumpus for so long ...

Tesh first, then Tash began to be aware of 'worry' somewhere in front of them. They must be getting quite close to home.

'We're nearly there,' gasped Tesh, the words coming out in a funny croaky voice. Nobody said anything. Every step was a battle. At last, there was a faint aroma in the air - wood smoke! More struggling steps. There was a sliver of light from a cottage window! They were coming to the edge of the forest!

The villagers had been having a meeting. In a small, close community like this, everyone was stricken with anxiety. Indalesh, the eldest and wisest, felt torn inside. Winter had hit fast. The storm had been severe; the village was deep in snow and now a bitter cold had set in. If the group were out in this, they might not survive. They should have been back by now. Had something happened to them? Had Thumpus turned nasty? Suresh had said that the beast should never have been brought in at all, least of all should they have sent a party out searching for him, risking their own lives. Other heads nodded.

Should they send out another party after the first? And would that be lost too, in the endless forest? Maybe they should have learnt more about these woods - then they wouldn't be so helpless in an emergency. But it was no use thinking that now ...

'Hey, hey, hey! Wake up! We're back!' There were strangled shouts outside. Everyone rushed for the door of the large hut that was the village meeting place. As they tumbled out, the light showed the little group staggering to a halt, snow-covered and dishevelled, Tash still on Thumpus' back, too tired even to get off. They had made it! It was Tesh's turn for the world to spin. Her legs gave way under her, and Lelesh caught her as she fell.

Indalesh had kept a fire going in Prush and Lelesh's cottage. They carried the children in and threw off their sodden clothes, fumbling with bootlaces to free icy feet. Thumpus crawled in after them, trying to be extra careful with his tail. Even he needed the warmth after the icy cold outside. He took up a whole corner of the room, dripping melting snow on to the floor.

The other villagers crowded in.

'What happened?'

'Are you alright?'

'Tell us about it!'

'We're all right. In the morning, in the morning! Thank God for Thumpus!' was all Lelesh could manage to say. After the door had closed, after they had all thawed out a bit, she had just enough energy left to tuck Tesh and Tash into their beds.

The Chronicles of Thumpus Wumpus

9.

Bees and tears

The days passed. The story was told and retold and Thumpus was everyone's hero. He spent a lot of time lying on his back being petted. There was not even a splash of another washing! He encouraged Tash's telepathic training; Indalesh discovered some small talent as well, though she had missed too many years to become really good. But nobody else seemed to have the ability. Thumpus could understand their thoughts, but they couldn't read his, or each others'.

The weather relented after the big freeze. In fact, it became positively balmy, as if atoning for the previous days of snow and cold. Prush and Lelesh were building a fine shed for Thumpus. Minesh and Tansh, grateful for their own rescue in the forest, lent a hand. It would be as large as a small room. Thumpus could spread himself out on the raised floor, above the cold ground, in unheard-of luxury. Somebody made a little sign saying 'Thumpus' Place' to nail by the door when it was finished - not that there was anyone who didn't know. Thumpus was extremely proud of his new abode and had to be cautioned by Tesh never to try to wump inside, or it would fall apart. His wumps, frequent now he was happy at being in the village, were carefully executed, away from vulnerable walls, fences and, especially, people.

There was not a person in the village who did not come to pay a friendly call on Thumpus, braving his musty odour - except Suresh. He had been doubtful about sending out the rescue party in the first place, and had been sure that Thumpus himself was responsible for its disappearance. Now, Tesh and Tash reluctantly performed the work promised in return for the tub of honey Thumpus consumed on his ill-fated first visit.

Suresh was single by long choice, grumpy and with a temper which, at times, could rival Kamal's. A good person to leave to himself. But Suresh was brilliant with bees. Bees, of course, give honey, and Thumpus was interested in honey, his favourite treat. So Thumpus stirred himself and went to watch Suresh working with his hives. Suresh was cleaning them out and making sure that just the right amount of honey was left for the bees in winter. He had 30 hives and passed his spare time making more, which he sometimes traded down the hill. He was the nearest thing to a businessman the village had. Most of his honey he exchanged with the villagers, which meant that many things were done for him. Still, he himself kept up a good garden as well as his hives. In his mind were plans for expansion of the honey business. There was an enormous demand for it among the people down the hill. If he could increase production, he could sell the honey there for a better price and make improvements to his house. For instance, you could actually get plated wood stoves now, with a proper hotplate for cooking. Such a stove would keep your place toasty warm using half the wood of an open fire. He thought of replacing his heavy earthenware crockery with fine china, and his rough clothes with fine linen.

Thumpus just sat at the edge of Suresh's patch and watched the fellow busy himself with his hives, smoking the bees, active again in the warm weather, to keep himself from being stung. Suresh pretended not to notice him. After a while Thumpus sent a small thought to the beekeeper, without expecting any answer. He would ask Tesh to ask Suresh for him later, when she had finished her lessons.

<Where get bees?> Thumpus wanted to know. To his astonishment, Suresh picked up the thought perfectly and sent an instant reply. The man was a superb telepath!

<Divide hives from time to time. Sometimes get wild swarms from forest.> Suresh thought just like Thumpus, in a kind of minimal language, wasting no words.

As Thumpus got over his surprise at Suresh's unsuspected talents, a plan began forming in his mind. Suresh wanted bees. Thumpus wanted honey. Because honey was a big thing for Thumpus, whenever he saw bees flying, he traced their direction home and quickly found their nests, some of which had probably escaped from Suresh's fold while swarming. Most of them were too high for him to get at, but he carefully remembered their location. Who knew when the information might come in useful? Now perhaps his meticulousness would pay off. Perhaps *with* Suresh, things could be different.

<Know many places where wild bees. You catch?>

Suresh looked up from his work at last. This was interesting.

<Can catch,> came the reply. <You take?>

<Honey? Yes!>

<I give you a tenth part all new hives I get through you.>

Thumpus knew the whereabouts of many nests. A tenth part of all the honey they'd produce would be quite a lot. But what about the rest? That was even more!

<Third part,> he countered, <me a third, you a third, bees a third.>

<Bees need half. Of rest I offer you two-tenths. Otherwise > Suresh sent a disgusting image. It quite shocked Thumpus. Being just an animal, he'd never been good at working out quantities - he hadn't needed to be.

<OK. Two-tenths.> That seemed like double what he had been offered - a good deal! Thumpus missed that the bees would get half, leaving him having exactly the same amount as

Suresh had offered in the first place. Suresh gave a broad grin. He hadn't grinned like that for ages. He could like this funny old Thumpus, who he could talk to without words. But could he deliver?

<When?>

<Tomorrow.>

At this time of year, it wasn't really possible to entice the bees to a portable hive. They were too sleepy to make the effort. But as soon as the sun was up, the pair set off. Thumpus told Tash and Tesh he was off to the woods for the day and, reluctantly, they let him go. It was a beautiful late autumn morning, the trees were majestic in dark green and the occasional bright yellow of a birch whose leaves had survived the snow undaunted. It was deeply still. Thumpus was in a wonderful mood. Suresh, his new-found abilities active, began to share it, in spite of his dour nature.

Thumpus knew that the bees did not nest in the heart of the pine forest, where there were no flowers. He was taking Suresh to an area of rocky outcrops unknown to the villagers about two hours' walk away to the north-east, where the pine trees were scattered, with more clumps of birch and plenty of flowers in spring and summer. There he knew of about ten nests. Others were farther away, more than a day's walk for Suresh, but this would do as a start.

Suresh was a sturdy walker and this time, in his mellow mood, he trusted Thumpus not to get him lost, even though they were going in an unfamiliar direction. Secretly, even he had been impressed by the tale of the rescue and the journey of the search party back to the village. He plodded along, while Thumpus almost danced in his joy at the warmth in the air. There would be few days like this before the spring. Soon the way became steeper, more uneven; they came to more or less open ground. There were still enough trees for bees to find nest holes. A rock-strewn burn danced across the land, sharing their mood.

<Now,> sent Thumpus, <honey spots.>

There were even a few bees still around, searching for a last touch of pollen. He led Suresh to a tree and there, about 5 metres up - too high for Thumpus to reach - was a hole with a large old nest. When he had come here at first he had tried sending its inhabitants away on a wild bees' chase, to pollen fields of unimaginable richness. But even with the guardians gone, he still couldn't access the honey, so he gave up taunting them. The bees, secure for now, grinned down at him - he was sure of it. But in the spring things would be different. Suresh gazed up, assessing the site with a practised eye, and marked the tree carefully, so only he would recognise the mark. There was no competition, but you couldn't be too careful. He would come back with light travelling hives when the bees were active again.

By lunchtime the pair had marked more than half of Thumpus' spots. They sat on rocks in a clearing by the stream. Suresh unwrapped a large piece of honeycomb and some black bread and gave some to Thumpus. He provided the food as the price of guidance and, although it hurt him, he did want to impress Thumpus with the quality of his honey. Thumpus was duly impressed and speedily demolished it.

<Wonderful honeycomb,> he sent. <Watch out, must have wump!> As Suresh hastily stood back, he swung his enormous tail and beat the ground, sending a roaring tremor through the woods. The more open ground magnified it.

Far, far away, so far across the mountains that you could hardly imagine it, another being who happened to be aware at the same time, picked up the faintest echo of the tremor, like a seismograph picking up a trace of a faraway earthquake. She knew what it was! Stunned, she returned her very loudest wump. There was no way that Thumpus could have heard it, but his telepathic brain registered the faintest *something,* at the very periphery of consciousness. He stood up excitedly and turned in the direction of the feeling. A female

Thumpus Wumpus! He had given up believing that one still existed - A mate ...

He looked towards the shimmering white-capped peaks, faintly visible in the early afternoon haze. She was beyond them, he knew it. And there he would have to go. It would be the mother of all journeys. No way he could do it before the spring. Even a Thumpus would not cross those mountains at this season of the year. When it got warm... He wumped again, a magnificent effort. Everything in his life was changing. Dear friends, a warm den for the snows to come, and now, potentially, a mate. Life was just wonderful.

Suddenly, Suresh, standing by - dour, sour, surly, angry Suresh - began to cry. Thumpus had not tried to disguise his feelings. He had sent with all the energy he possessed - and a tiny crack opened in Suresh's wizened old heart. His first sobs were like the creaking of a rusty gate, but soon, as they gained momentum, the tears ran and ran - a dam opened, a barrel breached. Thumpus looked on amazed, sensing the years of pain, loneliness and misery locked up inside that flinty old heart. Then, remembering his own state until so recently, he too began to howl, accompanying Suresh's heaving sobs. The bee man cried on and on, releasing an epoch of misery. With another human, he couldn't have done it, he was too proud. But Thumpus was an animal, not a person. He howled on and Thumpus yowled with him.

Far away in the village, everyone stopped what they were doing and looked up as strange echoes wafted across the trees. Tesh heard, inside, and was worried for a moment, but then, suddenly, her mood became almost euphoric. Nothing was wrong, really.

It seemed that Suresh would cry for days. The sun dropped low in the west. The location of the remaining bees' nests was forgotten. Thumpus nudged the still weeping Suresh.

<Must go now,> he sent. <Light gone soon.>

They trudged back through the woods. With the walking, Suresh's tears abated. The flood had opened a way to a Suresh locked away inside him almost since babyhood. For the first time in years he felt innocent, even hopeful. Things *could* be different. He looked gratefully at Thumpus, the unwitting cause of his release.

'What a wonderful animal,' he thought to himself. Thumpus heard. Such a thought from Suresh was praise indeed. He felt warm along his back fur. A picture of a grateful Suresh ladling out great spoonfuls of honey to Thumpus came to his mind and he hastily suppressed it, hoping Suresh hadn't noticed. Suresh, however, was too busy with his own new thoughts. As dark closed in they reached the edge of the village clearing.

The Chronicles of Thumpus Wumpus

10.
Thumpus' Place.

Prush and Lelesh continued to work hard on Thumpus' new winter quarters, making good use of the warm spell. Tesh and Tash helped. It was part of their education to learn how to build the kind of rough but comfortable wooden houses the villagers lived in and already Tash and Tesh were quite good carpenters, though they couldn't carry the big logs for the house by themselves. Amazingly, Suresh came a couple of times to help. Everyone commented on the change in him, and some suspected it was connected with the trip with Thumpus to find bees' nests. People thought even better of Thumpus - the village was a happier place when Suresh was in a good mood.

The other villagers didn't help with the house, apart from making encouraging comments - they were much too busy getting things organised for winter. Without freezers, food had to be bottled and pickled, or salted and preserved and the last vegetables harvested and stored. As well, wood needed to be cut and piled for winter fires, the gaps in timbers (revealed by the first cold spell) sealed with mud and moss, and winter clothes inspected for moth holes and patched. Also, Indalesh, who was not so physically capable as the others, had to be assisted so her house would be as cosy as possible for the winter. Luckily, Prush and Lelesh always made a point of getting as much done early as they could so they weren't behind in their tasks, even though Thumpus' appearance had been very distracting.

They built the new structure close to their own, so the houses could give protection to each other. There were no shops to buy timber from, so everything had to be cut down from the forest and then smoothed and notched into place with the other timbers. Since metal items had to be brought from the lowlands far away and cost an arm and a leg, they used the village's only wood drill to make holes in the notched beam ends and knocked wooden pegs in them to keep things together. The floor was simple beaten earth was carried in to raise it from the surrounding area with straw added to keep the cold at bay. The roof was hardest. Logs were notched to a central beam and pegged together. Lots of cuts, already made in them with an axe, held hundreds of small crosspieces. Turf was upturned on top. The final layer was birch bark, fixed in place from the bottom up.

The hut that emerged was much simpler than a house. Without a chimney, it was only one room, with quite a small roof, and a large opening, almost the whole of one end, facing the sunny side for Thumpus to get in and out comfortably. No Thumpus Wumpus had ever had such a house before. Winter in the mountain forests was cold, damp and unpleasant with little food, and shortened the life of many Wumpii. Thumpus saw the effort that was being made for him and tried to help, getting in the way and rolling on his back to be cuddled at crucial moments.

<Oh Thumpus, you bumbling old pot,> sent Tesh for the umpteenth time as she tripped up over the beast's tail, sending an armful of birch bark strips flying, <how can we finish your house if you keep getting in the way? Away with you and catch a rabbit or two for dinner.>

They had found that their new companion had one or two skills besides being warm and friendly. For one thing, he was a pretty good rabbit hunter, confusing the hapless creatures with inner messages till they more or less ran into his paws. There were plenty of rabbits around until the real cold descended on the forest, and Thumpus used to catch them and store them in special holes in old trees to eke out his winter diet. He didn't mind them a bit putrid - Wumpii have iron digestions. Now he brought them fresh to Lelesh to be hung, salted and stored, a much better plan.

Ruefully, he made for the woods. He was only trying to be supportive but they always sent him away. He concentrated on the nice winter house he would have, so as not to get resentful. After a while he forgot it all, engrossed in a game of delusion with the poor rabbit folk.

Although the work was hard, it was not long before Thumpus' rude hut was standing complete beside the family house, with a good layer of straw to supplement his shaggy fur. Suresh's help was invaluable. They realised he was a very good builder, probably the best in the village.

Thumpus crawled in, delighted, and wallowed in the fresh straw. This would be the best winter ever. Just what a Thumpus needed and deserved, next to good friends and companions. If he could have grinned, he would have done so. Instead, he crawled out, covered with straw like a scarecrow, cast a leery eye around the builders and raised his tail for a wump of appreciation.

<No!> yelled Tash suddenly, sending at the same time. <You'll knock the whole thing down!

<Do it over there,> he continued somewhat more gently, as the crestfallen Thumpus paused in mid-swipe.

'Can't do anything round here without being shouted at and pushed around,' thought the animal. 'What an awful winter it's going to be.' But running away again didn't enter his head. At least nobody tried to wash him any more - they seemed to be getting used to his BO.

The new hut had to be celebrated. Tesh and Tash built a big bonfire with all the bits and pieces of wood left over from building the hut and Indalesh prepared a big stew in her largest cook pot. As dusk brushed away the red sunset and the stars began to watch, the whole village gathered around the fire, everyone bringing something. Suresh was there, though normally he never came to celebrations. They formed in a semicircle around the new hut, young and old alike holding hands. There were only 23 people, but it was their community. Everyone closed their eyes. Indalesh, as the oldest, led the ritual.

'We appreciate this new hut,' she intoned. 'We appreciate the people who built it, the tools that they used, the forest that gave the wood, our special new animal friend, Thumpus, who will live in it, the shelter it will give, the sun and stars that will look down on it, the rain and snow that will fall on it, the earth which supports it, our village that surrounds it. Let us bless it as a new part of the mystery that enables everything to be created, to exist and to pass away.'

'Aye,' said everyone together. They squeezed hands, let go, opened their eyes and the simple ceremony was over. Thumpus' own eyes shone. He didn't understand the words, but he could feel the beauty of the blessing - like the moonshine in the silent forest, or sun glittering on the waters of a stream, or the white of snow-covered peaks far away against blue sky. A wump was essential. He backed away from the group to an open space and swung his tail. The earth resounded with a satisfying, releasing boom.

The fire was lit, food brought out, and then it was story-telling time. Since there were no televisions, no videos, and no cinemas, stories were very important, and the villagers were very good at telling them. You told stories to relive the important things that happened, and to keep them in your memory for the next generation. Your imagination took the words of the story and clothed them in images and pictures.

As the evening wore on and potatoes baked in the fire's ashes, the events of Thumpus' arrival were retold. Then Suresh indicated that he would like to speak. It was unprecedented - Suresh had never spoken at a story-telling. He had hardly ever even attended one. Hesitantly at first,he told the story of how he had arrived in the village, of why he had been so surly and miserable, and of how Thumpus had changed him. After he had finished, everyone was still for a long time.

And then Thumpus began to send a story to Tesh. It was the story of the wild woods where he had lived so long, of places and things there that the villagers didn't know about, and of many other things ...

Very late, after midnight, everyone reluctantly left the embers of the fire and went to their homes, children cuddling close to their parents. It was the last open-air story-telling of the year, because the weather changed next day: the cold set in and inside was the place to be. But these two stories were so special that they deserve to be retold, which is what I shall do next.

The Chronicles of Thumpus Wumpus

11.
The Stories.

'**W**e were out finding bees' nests for next spring,' began Suresh. Telling his story was hard, but if he was going to hold on to the new Suresh, the real Suresh, he had to share, at last, with his community. It was scary, but an intuitive feeling told him he would not be judged, that everyone would support him.

'It was a beautiful afternoon. Thumpus heard something far, far away that came from another Thumping Wumpus - a female. He was so happy. He thought of a mate in the spring, and dear friends and warmth and comfort over the winter, things he hadn't had before.'

'How did you know?' interjected someone.

'I seemed to be able to communicate directly with him, just like Tesh and Tash,' said Suresh. Tash was very pleased he had been included. His abilities were nowhere near as developed as Tesh's, but he was working hard at it.

'Feeling Thumpus' happiness, my heart opened at last, and I began to cry. It want on and on, for hours. Thumpus howled with me.'

People nodded: everyone in the village had sensed something that afternoon. Heads turned, appreciatively, to Thumpus.

'After that, I felt like a new person,' continued Suresh, 'so I want to share my story. It's a sad one,' he added, to prepare them.

'I was born in a village by the sea far, far away, many days' journey from here. It was a poor place and my parents were poorer than most - except in children. My mother had given birth to 12 - and 10 were living. I was the youngest one.'

There were gasps from the listeners. People in the village loved children, but it was unusual to have more than two or three. Rightly or wrongly, they felt that they could be cared for better that way.

'It was a rough life. I remember always being hungry, but I loved my parents and my brothers and sisters and they loved me. Perhaps I was spoiled because I was the youngest. We would play on the shore, mend nets and help Dad clean the fishing boat that gave us our food and what money we had. Dad caught fish; Mum sold them to everyone else.'

The older people in the village knew about sea fish. Once, a small basket of salted fish had been traded to the village for logs. They were smelly and tasted pretty bad, but it was winter and they were a useful addition to the limited diet. They had given people the idea of salting the small trout they caught in the streams nearby to preserve them for winter.

'One day, when I was about four, I think, people came from the town. They said we village folk had too many children and couldn't look after them properly. They said we would be better looked after by people in the town. So they grabbed us - all the younger ones. We ran away, but they caught us. They shoved us onto carts pulled by horses. They had to tie us in or we would have jumped out. Almost every family in our village lost children. Five were taken from our family. It was a terrible day, the worst day of my life - us kids screaming, parents weeping and trying to get to us, held back by soldiers with spears. Bundled up and tied into the carts in just the clothes we wore, we were taken off and away, no-one knew where. That was the last I ever saw of my family and my village.'

People gasped.

'Did you ever go back to find them?' asked Tansh. He could hardly believe people could do things like that to other people.

'How could I?' answered Suresh. 'The land down there is huge. There are hundreds and hundreds of villages like mine, and big, smoky towns, where people lived worse than we did.

'Anyway,' he continued, 'we travelled for days. All the time the group was getting smaller. I was the last of my family to be dropped off. It was in a town far down the hill, where there's a place, a Home for children whose parents have died or things like that. It was just horrible. The food was worse than even I had had and the water tasted foul, but you couldn't get ill or they beat you. Nobody really cared about you unless there was an inspection, when we were all dressed in smart clothes and given a good meal. After the inspector went away, things were as bad as before.

'I wanted to die, but something made me go on living. I kept quiet and tried not to be noticed. That way you didn't get beaten so much. But inside I was angry, full of rage at what they had done. So if I got the chance I did nasty things, cruel things. It seemed to help, but it didn't really. I spent years and years in that place. I grew up bitter and surly. The only thing that saved me was the bees. I used to watch them getting nectar from the flowers in the garden and going back to their nest. It reminded me of the big family I'd been part of.'

Suresh paused to wipe a tear from his eye. Several of the others were doing the same.

'When I got older I was apprenticed out to a carpenter. He was a hard man with no love for a stray child forced on him and it was not much better than the Home. But at least I learnt something useful from it. Finally, I left the Home; had to fend for myself. I got odd jobs that kept me alive.

'I was bitter from head to toe. The worst was, I was bitter to myself. I thought I was no good. I would probably have spent my life drinking and been in and out of jail, but one good thing happened. I was turning to stealing and the bottle when I did a job for a beekeeper, helping him build hives. He saw I loved the bees, that I had a way with them, and he offered me work helping mind them. He had hundreds of hives, too many for him alone. He was mean enough, but being with the bees was about the only thing I liked. With them, I didn't feel so bad. I despised humans, yet I could live with bees!

'So I went on. It was a lonely and unhappy life. I was grumpy and miserable to the rest of the world, but the bees gave me peace. I wandered from place to place, staying here and there for a while, getting farther and farther from the home I was brought up in. Finally, I got as far as I could go, which was here, where the endless forest begins. You were kind enough to give me a place as a beekeeper, I built my hut and lived my surly years.

Now things have changed, thanks to Thumpus. He gave me hope in a hopeless world, tears in eyes that had forgotten them, and I realise what a very good, special place this is. I thank you for putting up with me till now. And I'm sorry!'

As Suresh finished his sad tale there were tears in the eyes of the villagers. Many moved to hug him and he started to cry again. But this time the tears were of happiness, of acceptance and transformation. Eventually, Suresh went to his house and brought a big jar of honey to share with everyone.

Things settled down. All now turned to Thumpus. The hairy beast shifted a bit, looking at people with sidelong glances from his big brown eyes. He knew they wanted a story from him, but, being only an animal, he couldn't speak. He looked at Tesh, and Tesh nodded, with shining eyes. She would translate his thoughts and images into human words.

This was what she said on Thumpus' behalf:

'I am from the long woods,' she translated, 'the woods that go on for ever, or almost. The woods that surround the white mountains far away.

'None of you know the woods. None of you have explored them. I hope you will one day, but do not bring the towns Suresh talked about to the woods, for they are too precious.

Among the trees I was often lonely. Thumping Wumpii are the rarest of the animals and I never met another. The trees gave me comfort. Even now I am with you and no longer lonely, I must go back to the woods often. That is my belonging place.

'The trees are living beings, but they are not like humans or animals. They are like ants or bees - collective.' Thumpus gave a warm glance to Suresh, who was clearly following his story inwardly, not hearing Tesh's words. 'They are aware enough, but they can't move or act; the Wood Beings organise and control them, beings that only inner eyes can see. They care for the smaller animals that you know.

Around here, the woods are very quiet. The big animals keep away from where you humans live. The nearest is Kamal.' Tesh's voice shook a little as she mentioned the name. 'There are more of his kind in the woods, as well as his smaller relatives. Farther away begin the ones that run in packs. They are fast, but not so large. Sometimes when they are happy and enjoy the moon, they howl a bit - like me.'

Thumpus leered round - in a human, it would have been a smile.

'They eat the ones with horns, the big, gentle grass-eaters. Farthest away are the most fearful of all, the striped ones, who hunt very quietly, and are clever. Beware of the striped ones. Only a Thumping Wumpus can deceive them, but even we keep out of their area, for now we are few, very few.'

Thumpus stopped sending for a moment, thinking of *how* few. At least there was one other - if she survived till spring. Then he continued, via Tesh:

'There is also the Great Being.'

As she continued to translate, Tesh gasped at the image.

'It lives high in the mountain and it flies, though it is huge. Its tail is longer than mine and it breathes fire, which all the animals and the trees fear most. Only rocks enjoy that. It is the guardian of all, forest and mountain, river and clearing, animal, fish and insect. It understands all of them, and all bow down to it. It was not born, it does not die, nor does it get older. It speaks with the beings of the woods and organises everything in its own way. I have only seen it only once, from far away. It is awesome. I can't be sure if I saw it in my head or outside.'

There was a long silence as people tried to take the words in.

'What about thumps?' someone said after a while. 'Tell us about them.'

Thumpus cast a hard look at the speaker. He didn't like the term 'thump'; it did not show proper respect to a Thumping Wumpus.

It was Rensh, husband of Wilash, and the father of three young children, Nilish, Sharish and Varsh.

'Young and inexperienced,' thought Thumpus disparagingly. Tesh did not translate, but Suresh smiled and Tash giggled.

Nevertheless, he politely answered Rensh.

'Thumping Wumpii are the oldest of the animals, apart from the Great Being,' Tesh went on translating. 'The story is that we were once the agents of the Great Being, who needed help to get things organised at the start of time. That is why we can read and send thoughts - to communicate with him. As time went on and things mostly looked after themselves in the forest lands, we gradually became fewer and fewer. There are hardly any of us left now. We are gentle, peaceable creatures, eating only roots and plants.'

At this point Tesh and Suresh both looked hard at Thumpus. There was no doubt that he enjoyed the odd rabbit, mouse, grub and any other small animal or insect that gave him half a chance to eat it. Thumpus stared blandly at them over the ring of rapt listeners around the fire.

<You old ratbag!> sent Tesh. <You're pretending to be an angel and you aren't one at all!>

<Angel?> was all the sneaky old beast returned.

'Go on, Tesh!' said someone. 'Is something wrong?'

Tesh sighed. He was incorrigible. Thumpus began sending again.

<Gentle and peaceable,> Thumpus reiterated, and Tesh carried on translating. 'We are actually sociable animals, but now there are so few of us, we are mostly alone. Sometimes we never meet another of our kind. But the woods are our friends and we usually outwit the violent animals and send them in the other direction while we get out of the way. We rarely come to any harm from them. With our wumps and howls we give voice to the joy of the woods.'

'Why do you wump mostly at night?' asked Minesh.

'Because the woods come alive at night,' translated Tesh. 'You sleep at night. We sleep any time, but as the sun goes down, the trees wake up and the tree spirits begin to move among them. You must have noticed how strong the trees are then.'

Everyone nodded. The woods *did* get stronger and spookier as the dusk grew. The young ones shivered. There were tales of the ghosts and strange beings haunting the forest when the dark closed in.

'It is wonderful to be with the trees when the full moon dapples silver and shadow over everything, when a breeze shifts the branches. Everything shimmers in the woods then - who wouldn't want to give a wump?' Thumpus sent the image so strongly that everyone picked it up. It *was* scary, but incredibly beautiful.

'In the spring,' Tesh took up Thumpus' final images 'come with me to the woods. There may be a time when you will have to come, for the lands that Suresh spoke of are greedy. Soon they will exhaust the woods they still have. Then they will come here and cut and cut and cut. To stay happy, we will have to travel far.'

These last words shocked everyone. Thumpus had lifted his head and closed his eyes. Even he was not sure where the thoughts had come from. Nobody wanted to hear them. Life was good at the edge of the woods. Few people came, few people left. The awful world of Suresh's story seemed far away. Slowly, talking quietly to themselves, people got up and drifted away to their houses. Thumpus' words had put a questionmark over their lives. The storytelling was over.

The Chronicles of Thumpus Wumpus

12.
To Find a Mate

All had departed for bed, leaving Thumpus after many strokings and cuddles. Tesh and Tash were very moved. They had experienced his story directly, especially the strange energy that surrounded Thumpus' last words.

The last embers died. Like other animals, Thumpus had an aversion to fire, but he realised that humans seemed to live by it, cooking things, warming their hairless skins. He was getting used to it.

Thumpus entered his new house to sleep for the first time. He was not sure where the thoughts that had ended his description of his forest home belonged. He was afraid they had come from the Great Being itself. He had shared that Thumping Wumpii had been the agents of the Great Being in bygone ages. So his mother had shared with him. But he had never had such a message before, as if a warning was being given. He didn't want to be a messenger of bad news. He settled on the fresh straw, snuggling in to make a nest in it. This, at least, would be a good winter. Normally he would have been wakeful. Tonight, exhausted after the evening, his head went between his paws and he slept.

Tesh slept too. After a while she began to dream. In her dream there were people in the village, lots of them, ignoring the villagers, cutting down trees, making great swathes through the forest. Everywhere there was noise, dirt and smoke. A group of men with big carts came out of the smoke, grabbed Thumpus and put chains on his legs. For all his struggles he could do nothing and was dragged off into one of the carts. Tesh screamed and screamed at the men but they paid her absolutely no attention at all. She awoke to find Tash shaking her shoulder.

'Tesh, you'll wake the whole place! What's the matter?'

'Had a nightmare.' Tesh found herself shivering. 'Tell you in the morning.' If she shared it now, Tash might start getting nightmares too. 'Go back to sleep.'

For a long time Tesh lay awake, troubled. The village was quiet. No-one would come up here in the winter, anyway. Slowly, she drifted off to sleep again.

The winter passed. It was not the worst they had known, nor the gentlest. Sometimes the snow lay deep, at other times it melted away in a brief mild spell. Thumpus became accepted as a village resident. People even got used to his smell. On mild nights he ventured out to check the woods; mostly, he lay around and got a lot of petting from the children of the village. He was still especially close to Tesh and Tash. Tash found that, with practice, he could understand thoughts better - but only from Thumpus. He and Tesh could not communicate together without words, nor with Suresh, who often visited to exchange thought pictures with Thumpus. Indalesh could sometimes understand Thumpus, but had trouble sending her own thoughts, though Thumpus picked up more than he let on. No-one else in the village seemed to have the ability.

Gradually, the days began to lengthen. The trees thought of spring, the plants and animals picked it up: green appeared on the forest floor and bird song echoed around. Thumpus was restless. Every night he went to the woods, ranging from the edge of Kamal's territory to the beehive glades and beyond, in the direction of the white mountains. Sometimes he would be away for two or three days at a time. He explained it was to get rid of his winter fat, but Tash and Tesh were sure something else lay behind it. Suresh just nodded and went on making hives, laboriously cutting boards till he'd used all his precious screws and nails, and begged for more around the village. The sun lifted its head and shone warm between rain showers.

In Thumpus' mind was the vague tremor the earth had brought him last autumn, the tremor that meant the possibility of a female of his species somewhere beyond the faraway mountains. He made his most massive wumps in the clearing where he had felt the vibration before, but could sense nothing in return. It seemed crazy to set out without the slightest indication that he had been right all those months ago. He began to lose weight, wandering restlessly, always shifting a little towards the high peaks far away.

It was on a still night, with the full moon overhead making magic of the woods, that he finally heard it. A sound, or tremor, so distant that it might have been wishful thinking rather than reality. A wumping sound, the sound of a female Thumping Wumpus pleading for a mate. Thumpus knew he must go, there and then. What if there were another male Wumpus in range of that faint call? He became a bundle of instincts. He must be there first. But before he was torn away to the far distance, he sent his strongest thought back to the village.

<Seeking mate. Back one day.> It was Tash who picked up the thought. He often slept restlessly at full moon, and was lying staring at the pale light at the window and the shadows it made in the room. He woke Tesh without hesitation.

'Tesh, Tesh, wake up! Thumpus has gone. He sent a message from far away. He's looking for a wife. He sent he'd be back sometime.' Tesh, half-asleep, groaned. A sense of foreboding filled her. Everything was going to change now.

The message sent, nothing could hold Thumpus back. He didn't know if anyone had heard, but he just couldn't think any more about that. Gone was the tame Thumpus of the fireside, sharing thoughts with human friends. He had become a wild Thumpus of the woods, all alertness and energy. He could almost feel the last of the winter fat shedding from him as he moved at a brisk pace past thicket and clearing. Yes, a Thumpus could move in a way no humans could match. He was almost happy to have left. He was free!

The kilometres passed under his endlessly padding feet. As the sun took over watch from the moon, he took a short nap and a drink. Then he was on his way again till he was far beyond the area he had roamed in the last few years. Yet he had come this way once, he was sure. Perhaps the Great Being assigned the thumping wumpii to different areas of the forest as caretakers and sent them out to do their work. For a moment he pictured the Being, high in the mountains, a dragon of dragons. The Being seemed uneasy, and he let the thought go, concentrating all his energy on the journey ahead.

The land rose; boulders were sprinkled between the pines; through the trees the white mountains shone a little nearer. As night fell, Thumpus remembered hunger; there was a rotting log filled with grubs, a carpet of wood sorrel to graze. Wood sorrel was good. He moved on. There was plenty of water from the melting snows in rivulets everywhere. Sometimes he had to leap a stream and, occasionally, to jump from rock to rock across a torrent. The moon shone fitfully; at its highest, Thumpus sensed the call again, half-sound, half-feeling: <Come.>

<Coming!> he returned, fatigue forgotten, and was off again through the trees and rocks.

As day followed day, it snowed lightly, then drizzled, and the wind blew cold. Still Thumpus pressed on, picking up morsels to eat when he could. He was growing really thin. He felt as if his skin was a coat the humans put on, loose where the fat had been. Once a pack of hunters, the wolves, sensed him and showed interest. He sent an image of a group of horned ones, elk, far off to the left and the wolves turned away in haste. He caught a hare by chance and gobbled it down.

Once he came across a patch of good roots. But he didn't spend time hunting for food. The sense of another was stronger now.

In the foothills of the mountains he was skirting there were obstacles. Fast-flowing mountain rivers ran down, some of them too wide to jump. Much as Thumpus disliked it, he swam the icy waters. Even in his haste, he had to stop and wander up and down the banks till he found places where he would not be swept away. Still he went on, peaks always to his right, the land falling away steeply to the left. Once he came to a deep, sheer-sided gorge, with a big torrent boiling far below. Then he had to detour kilometres up river till he could leap perilously from rock to rock across the melee of waters. He was becoming aware of a deep exhaustion, but he still pushed himself onward.

In the end he had to sleep - his feet were faltering under him, dangerous in such rough country. He found a rock shelf which might give him some protection from predators and curled up. It was early afternoon. When he awoke, the moon was shining, the night well begun.

<Well,> came a thought into his head, <I to you; you to me. Find you sleeping at end. Maybe you too dozy to be right one.>

Thumpus snapped awake. He was cornered! His special place was a trap. He gave his best growl and prepared to fight to the end. Then he realised - the communication was inside. Another Wumpus! She must be the one he sought!

<Tired,> he sent back. <Too far travel without rest. Who?> he continued simply.

<Males always tired. No stamina.> Suddenly he made her out, at the edge of the rock shelf. Her odour was irresistible.

<Will have to do. No other contact.>

As Thumpus came fully awake he realised his blessing. At the end of his strength, she had found him! He knew he should strike the right pose, be strong and masterful - but the master was his stomach. A dreadful, empty ache there dominated every other feeling. Now that his quarry had been found, all that had been suppressed to get to her welled up.

<Starving,> he sent out involuntarily.

<Of course. First thought - sleep. Second thought - food. How long since mate?>

<Never,> Thumpus had to admit.

She was silent a moment.

<Journey?> she asked, more gently.

<Whole moon. Fast.>

<More than half a moon.> She didn't send, <fast> but he sensed she'd moved as quickly as he had. <Heard across one and a half moons. Where are Wumpii? All gone?>

<Only mother ever seen; everything learnt from her.> The two animals looked at each other, realising the extremity of their isolation. As they looked, a bond formed between them. Thumpus knew she would not leave if he ate.

<Three seasons no mate,> she sent, sadness in her sending. <Pupless, lonely.>

<Found 'humans',> he returned. <Friendly, loving. Some inside-speak. Live with.> He sent pictures, of Tesh and Tash, all surrounded with love; of Suresh, lonely like Thumpus; of all the others, with their pink skins covered in clothes; of the village, of his house. She was amazed, could hardly believe it.

<Real? Strange animals. Maybe something like beyond my area. Will check on return.>

<Real!> he confirmed, and then, urgently, <Food? Hungry!>

<Eaten. Good roots.> She sent an image of lots of them, maybe an hour away. Could he get there? He'd have to!

Thumpus stood up and stretched, trying to be nonchalant, to give a good impression. She thought he was a skinny wreck, but suppressed it. Maybe food and a bit of rest would improve him.

Every muscle he had seemed to be aching at once. He stretched again, as if to draw strength from the air, and moved towards her.

<Take to food?> he asked lamely.

<Poor old thing,> she returned, sarcastic again. <Yes, take.>

It was just 15 kilometres, but it seemed the longest journey he'd ever made. She led the way, often looking back pityingly on him. He knew her dilemma - he was her only chance, but he was so unfit, maybe not fit enough to give her a cub. Now that he'd stopped, he realised how soft he'd become over the winter.

Eventually they reached a large clearing. It was an ocean of roots. He'd never seen so many together. His mood changed. Happily he started scratching at the earth. Later, full up, he slept. When he woke, hungry again, his new partner was nowhere to be seen. Day was breaking. He wumped gently. No answer. He wumped again, loudly, anxiously.

<Over here,> she sent imperiously. She was downwind of him, only a few hundred metres away, but had masked her thoughts. While he slept, she had found a wild bees' nest in a rotten stump, and her claws and teeth opened it up as the bees searched for a heavenly meadow elsewhere. There was even some honey over for Thumpus. Perhaps she had deliberately left it. Perhaps she cared after all? He licked it up gratefully. She came up to him, nuzzling alongside him, open and receptive. He had some energy now. They mated and were happy together.

The Chronicles of Thumpus Wumpus

13
Unwelcome visitors

At the village, Thumpus was not just missed by those closest to him. His good-natured, easygoing manner had endeared itself to all. The people were intrigued by his journey and wondered what the outcome would be. Tash and Tesh were confident that Thumpus would return. They speculated that he might be accompanied by a wife, perhaps even by an adorable baby Thumpus as well.

At first, life went on as usual, but not long after the departure of their new friend, unexpected visitors arrived at the village from downhill. Although there was no road to the village, somehow three carts pulled by pairs of sweating horses managed to get there, the drivers using locally unknown words as they struggled to get over rocks, roots and boggy patches. Almost everybody not away working turned out for their arrival. It was a first for many people who had never seen a cart before. Since there were no roads and little transport, feet or, at best, a horse sufficed for the villagers' needs.

The carts pulled to a halt just before the houses. Suresh creased his brow, instantly worried at the implications of the unexpected arrival. Other adults held back, not wanting to seem too curious, but the children were excited by the diversion. They wanted to pet the huge cart horses, but were shooed away by the drivers.

'Little savages,' said one to his mates as they tended the animals. 'There'll be some changes made here, alright.' The others nodded. One spat openly on to the ground, the other pulled out a tube from his pocket, lit it, coughing and blew smoke all around, laughing as the children, who had never seen a cigarette before, backed off. Meanwhile, a portly man in very fancy clothes dismounted clumsily from one of the carts. This was truly the end of the world, he thought, eyeing the rough huts, the goat pens and the line of forest beginning just beyond the village cluster.

'Children,' he said imperiously, 'take me to the village headman.'

Tesh and Tash could feel the contempt behind the words. Same feeling came from the others.

'We don't have a headman,' Tesh took it on herself to reply, as the oldest child present. 'We decide big things together. But Indalesh is the oldest and wisest.'

'No matter,' returned the man. Tesh thought of him as 'Porky'. 'Take me to him.'

Tesh and Tash left the group of children gawping at the horses and took the man over to Indalesh's place. She had come out to see the carts struggling up the hill, but had returned to her house as they arrived. It felt better.

'Indalesh, there's a man wants to see you,' cried Tash, running ahead and knocking at the door. Indalesh came out and stood at the threshold. The bad feelings she was having instantly centred on the man approaching her. He stopped about 2 metres away, looking disdainfully.

'Woman, take me to your husband,' he said.

'My husband is long dead. I am Indalesh, elder of this village,' she replied, with a touch of pride. 'What can I do for you?'

The man stepped back, a little startled. 'A woman!' he said, under his breath. Then he stepped forward again.

'The Grand Archduke, blessed be his name -' he began importantly, but Indalesh interrupted him.

'You must be tired after your journey,' she said. 'Would you like a cup of tea? Come in.'

The man hesitated. Then he nodded and entered the house after her. 'Placate the natives,' he thought. 'No harm in creating a good impression.' The children followed.

For the first time, Tesh found herself aware of what was going on in another human being's head. 'Perhaps because he is so strange to us,' she thought. She had never considered understanding human thoughts before; she had thought she could only communicate with Thumpus like this. This man seemed to regard them as some sort of insect. Tash fidgeted beside her. He seemed to be suppressing anger. Perhaps he was reading the man's thoughts as well. He had come on a lot before Thumpus left.

Indalesh had water on the hob and made an infusion of hyssop and honey for them all. The man thought, 'Why are these children here? I must send them away.' Tesh picked it up easily, and suddenly decided to try something else new, something she had watched Thumpus doing with Kamal.

<Children very important,> she projected. <Should stay!>

Indalesh suddenly looked hard at her. The man looked uncomfortable. Nobody said anything out loud, though Tash suppressed a giggle, hastily turning it into a cough. Indalesh handed a mug of tea to each of them.

'Ahem,' the man began again, 'the Grand Archduke is expanding his Empire. He is going to incorporate your lands into it. This will bring many blessings to you and the village. I have come to survey what there is of value here for him. He instructs you to co-operate fully with me.'

'What are these blessings?' asked Indalesh. 'In general, we are very satisfied with our lives.'

'The blessings are innumerable. For instance, you will no longer be isolated. We will bring roads so you can travel down the hill. There will be proper education for the children, advanced tools for cutting the forest, modern weapons to protect you from wild animals, police to protect you from crime.

You will be able to earn money and there will be many more people to - be with,' he ended lamely. This was not going quite as smoothly as he had envisaged.

'Hmmm,' said Indalesh. 'We are relatively happy here, you know. We do have traders come to the village from time to time, and some people from villages down the hill have moved here to live. If we wanted a different lifestyle, we would have gone down, I think.'

'It is the wish of the Grand Archduke - blessed be his name - that all his citizens benefit from the progress his reign brings. You also.'

Indalesh sighed. 'We had better bring all the villagers together this evening. Then you can put your proposals to them and see what they think. I will ask them to build a fire.'

'In the meantime, I will survey the area's resources.'

He got up and left the cottage, as if with relief. 'Primitive,' he thought to himself. 'But this will become the centre for the exploitation of the inner forest.'

Tesh and Tash picked the thought up.

'That's what he's really about,' said Tash excitedly. 'Cutting down the trees. It'll be the end of us.' Tesh shuddered, remembering her dream.

'Indalesh, I had a dream that this was going to happen. A terrible dream. But there was more to it. They captured Thumpus and sent him off downhill in a cart, all chained up.'

'Don't worry, dreams can be wrong, or only partly right.' Indalesh tried to be soothing, but she was worried herself. 'You picked up his thoughts, didn't you?' She looked down at the children. 'And, Tesh, you tried to influence him so he'd let you stay. That is something very dangerous.' She wanted to say, 'You must never use it,' but she amended it to, 'You must never use it, unless you are in extreme danger.'

For the rest of the day, the stranger wandered about the area. He had lunch on a white cloth which was pulled out of a box in one of the carts by a driver - chicken and beef sandwiches, with a tomato - something the villagers never saw. They eyed him inquisitively, trying not to appear too interested. He ignored them. Meanwhile, rumours sped around the village, sourced from Tesh and Tash and spread by the other children. Indalesh decided to wait. Whatever story he gave in the evening, they could supplement it now.

The man made sketches on a big pad - sketches of the houses, of the fields, of the pens for the goats, of the forest edge. He walked into the woods a little way, as if to make sure that they were real. Then he walked along the line of trees this way and that, as if to measure how far they went. Once, nearing Suresh, busy with his bees, he asked, 'How far do the woods go?'

'Forever,' said Suresh shortly. He had not tried to read the man's thoughts, but he knew the purpose of the man's visit perfectly well. All their lives were going to change, and not for the better.

The man took his supper from the same white cloth, carefully unfolded, and drank from a bottle of wine. As darkness fell, a fire was lit at the village centre and the people gathered round it, sitting in a semicircle. The man took his time, but eventually he got up and approached. The drivers stayed by the carts.

'So few,' he thought. 'Less than two dozen. And they let their children come.' He remembered that the children had stayed during his meeting with Indalesh. Now why had he allowed that? It hadn't seemed a problem at the time. Perhaps nothing was important to these people, so they didn't bother to keep the children away.

At the meeting, he said just what he had said to Indalesh. And then, hesitantly at first, questions started to come:

'How many people will come?'

'Where will they live?'

'How will they be fed?'

'What will they do?'

'Will the trees be cut down?'

'How many?'

'For how far?'

He tried to be noncommittal, vague, to turn the conversation back to the benefits of being fully incorporated into the Grand Duke's Empire, but the damned fools seemed only to be interested in the protection of their miserable, primitive way of life.

'What will become of us?' murmured someone at the back of the firelight. It was half a rhetorical question.

With just a touch of exasperation, the man replied, 'You will experience all the benefits of the civilisation the Grand Duke has established and then you'll see how different life can be. You will be able to travel to the great cities on the new roads the Duke will build. You will be able to have modern medicine, instead of the quaint herbalism and mumbo jumbo you now use.' (He did not know what they now used for medicine, but assumed it must be that.) 'Your children will be able to go away to have the highest education, and if they are very clever, they may be able to serve the Grand Duke himself. You will be under the protection of his armies.' After he finished, there was a long silence.

Suresh, listening, felt he wanted to speak, to shout out a warning, a protest. But he kept quiet. This man, at least, would go away, and there would be a breathing space before the rest started coming. Tash, Tesh and Indalesh sat, silent like the others, beside the fire. Suddenly Suresh realised that they were projecting a message to him, like Thumpus: <Don't say anything. Wait.>

The man in front of them now seemed ill at ease.

'Are you not full of joy at the opportunities that are opening to you? Are you not eager for the changes, the opportunities, you will have?' he asked almost querulously.

'We will wait and see,' said Indalesh. 'Thank you for coming to inform us of this. Let us know if you require anything for your comfort.'

Any other visitor to the village would have instantly been invited to spend the night in one of the houses. But this man was different. They wanted him to go, so they could talk.

'So be it,' said the man. 'Upon reflection you will see how much benefit these changes will bring to you. I know for simple villagers it is a great deal to take in all at once,' he ended cuttingly.

'Good night,' they said politely, as he turned to go.

He barely nodded. He felt frustrated, even though he knew that once the Grand Duke heard his report of how enormous the forest was, a huge new industry would be established here. Those stupid villagers ought to appreciate the benefits of civilisation, compared to the primitive life they were living. Some of those children might have a spark of brain in them; perhaps one or two could even get an apprenticeship in the town. He turned and went back to his wagons. A tent was produced and erected. After ablutions he entered it and closed the flaps. The glow from an oil lamp lit up the canvas.

Now the villagers could talk alone. Clearly, as far as the man was concerned, they had no options. Suresh spoke at length. He had seen the way the man was examining the forest and asking questions about it. He knew what down the hill was like. Hundreds of people would come in. A timber mill would be built. The peaceful atmosphere of the village would be destroyed. Their way of life would be at an end. Rensh thought that there could be advantages - schools for the children, new things to buy. Anyway, they couldn't do anything about it. No-one had a piece of paper saying that they owned their land. If they objected, it might just be taken away. Tesh caused a sensation by saying that she had been able to read the man's thoughts, like Thumpus did. She told them of the man's contempt for the village and its occupants.

'I think they'll take our land away whether we like it or not and probably knock down our houses too,' she concluded.

The discussion went back and forth till late in the evening, everybody repeating themselves, as people do when they are deeply worried. Even Tash spoke up.

'We should pack up and leave,' he said.

'Where to?' said someone. Tash waved vaguely in the direction of the woods.

'Somewhere far away, where they won't find us.'

Nobody was ready to think of moving just because of the visit of one man. In the end they decided to do nothing at all for the time being - just to wait and see.

In the morning, breakfast was served on the white cloth, the tent was loaded into the cart and the visitors trundled away back down the hill. The drivers had hardly spoken a word to anyone, the man said no goodbyes, and the villagers, usually welcoming and polite, gave none either. 'Primitive *and* unfriendly,' thought the man. For some reason he was angry with these stubborn people who refused to see the advantages of progress. 'They've got it coming to them alright!' he thought.

For a few weeks, nothing happened. Village life returned to normal. Crops grew, weeds were cleared, goats kidded, the last winter supplies were opened. The sun shone and the rain fell. It was after a day of particularly heavy showers that the man's words began to come true. Towards evening, there was noise down the hill - shouting, banging, clattering and rumbling. A long procession of wagons and people was struggling through the muddy land up the hill towards the village. Horsemen in spattered uniforms, with whips and weapons rode around it. Carts were getting bogged in the mud. People swore. Whips were cracked and plied at horses.

Eventually, at what seemed a snail's pace, the carts managed to beat the mud and arrived at the village. They stopped on some grassy land, just outside. There were sixteen of them, driven by rough-looking men. About eight men were on horseback, clearly in control.

All the villagers watched. As the carts ground to a halt, Indalesh went over to one of them and spoke to the driver.

'Welcome,' she said. 'Who are you? Why are you here?'

'Better ask one of them, old woman,' he replied, rough, but not unfriendly, pointing at one of the riders. 'They take the decisions round here. We just do what we're told.'

She turned, as a horseman bore down on her. He was middle-aged, greying at the temples, with sad, cynical eyes. He had a sword at his belt and a whip coiled at the back of his saddle. 'You must be the headwoman we were told about. Well, we're the advance party to prepare camp for the woodcutters. You people got any food? Our supplies are rubbish. We'll give good money for it.'

'We don't use money much,' returned Indalesh. 'And it's a bad time for supplies. New crops are not ready yet,' she added, though any country person would have known why. 'But I'll see what I can do.'

The man nodded, turned and rode off. There was no request for permission to camp, no query if the location was all right. They just did what they wanted. Indalesh sighed. The cart driver, now dismounted and unhitching the horses, seemed to understand.

'That's how it is,' he said bleakly. 'I told you.'

Indalesh returned to the village and did her best to persuade people to spare some supplies for the newcomers.

'Whoever they are, we can at least be hospitable,' she said. 'Besides, it's best to show willing.'

But the people were not willing. They hadn't been warned or consulted. Food was scarce. Suresh flatly refused to give anything. Instead, he advised everyone to find hiding places for food.

'Soon they'll start taking, without a by-your-leave.'

Indalesh sighed again. She was afraid Suresh was right.

The new group was noisy and rowdy, but at least the grey-haired commander kept them in check. They put up tents, and began cutting great swathes of the forest to erect big huts, which, they said, were to be for the workers. They also said that another group was working to build a track but were starting at the other end, about three hours' walk away downhill where the nearest road ended. The villagers watched them, more and more frightened for the future of their home, aghast at the way the woods that were so much part of their lives were being treated. Indalesh had persuaded some people to supply milk from their goats. It was the only thing they had in surplus. Payment was given, but no-one was happy. Normally, that milk would be made into cheese and stored away. There was not enough for all the men, anyway.

After a day or two, Rinesh, coming back from milking the goats, was attacked and his milk pail stolen. He came home howling, scared out of his wits, and his mother, Nashe and Indalesh went to the grey man, as they had come to call the commander. The culprit was found, still with the bucket and, to the horror of the villagers, was publicly whipped the next day, squealing like a pig as the lashes cut. The children were hastily taken away to the houses. Tesh and Tash had to go to bed and be comforted, the thoughts and feelings coming from the man were so horrible. Nobody could believe that humans could do such things to each other. After that, an adult always went milking with the children which meant that other jobs didn't get done.

'If this is their civilisation, they can keep it,' Indalesh thought bitterly. But Suresh said there was worse to come.

The Chronicles of Thumpus Wumpus

14.
Thumpus returns

There *was* worse, much worse. As the weeks passed, the track was completed and with it came more and more workers. They lived in the barracks built by the first group, and started to devastate the forest in earnest. They made fires of brushwood which polluted the air. Stinking latrines were built. Goats began to disappear. There were fights. The children were too frightened go out in the evenings, when work finished. The villagers clustered together in their houses, afraid. The Porky man returned and began measuring out sections of woodland. Tansh, who went out to cut a tree for repairs to his hut, was arrested by the soldiers for 'cutting the Grand Archduke's wood'. However, the grey man showed some understanding and Tansh was released with a caution. It was allowed to take brushwood for fires, he was told, but all trees belonged to the Duke. Tansh returned shaken, minus his axe, to an hysterical Minesh.

Porky came to see Indalesh. A work camp wasn't a good environment for children, he said. He could arrange for them to be taken to the town, where they could get the sort of education they needed. Then they could get jobs as they grew older. The parents would not have to pay. This was the Grand Duke's generosity. Indalesh stalled him as best she could. They needed time. It was a new idea: give them a few weeks.

The people began to talk more and more of leaving, but where? Everywhere down the hill was the same. It looked as if the operation would go for kilometres and kilometres along the forest edge. Everyone was unhappy, and the precious crops were being trampled and taken. What would happen in the winter?

The two Thumping Wumpii were happy. They ran and played, hunted and grubbed for roots, sought out bees' nests and deceived their occupants. Thumpus felt like a baby Wump again. But, all too soon, the moment he knew somewhere deep inside him would happen, came.

<Baby Thumpus coming,> sent his partner. <Must return to homeland. You home, too.>

She moved away from him. It was the way wumpii were, had always been. After mating, when the female was sure she was pregnant, each animal returned to their own territory. Thumpus had never known his father, and now it looked as though he would never know his own baby. But Thumpus had been with humans, had seen new ways.

<I come too. Help with young one. Too few of us now. Need different ways,> he sent desperately. She looked at him. Was there some interest in her eyes?

<But forest to look after. Your job, my job - why we are here. Otherwise, maybe ...> - she began to move away, wasting no time - <The Great Being bless.>

<The Great Being bless.>

She was gone, a shadow moving away through the trees. She *was* interested, thought Thumpus. Perhaps that was why she had to go so fast, so as not to weaken. His world fell apart. He sat for a long time, tongue hanging out. The dusk began, the forest came alive. But still Thumpus sat. He felt as if he would never get up again. Darkness fell.

<Thumpus!>

Who called his name? Was he awake or asleep? There was a light around him - had he opened his eyes?

The Great Being of the mountains was before him, a huge dragon, green-scaled, breathing soft flames.

<You must go back, Thumpus. You're a people-Thumpus now. The people need you - Tesh, Tash, Suresh, the others. Woods up to here will go. Your work there will end. The people are part of the forest. Bring to safety, where Mate lives.>

Thumpus laid his head on the ground, utterly overwhelmed.

<Lord. How? What?> He couldn't think.

<Go! Do! Be very careful. Blessing on you.>

The presence, or vision, faded. Thumpus found himself prostrate in the small clearing. There was no dragon, but a beautiful smell, tinged with smokiness. He got up, stretched, and padded off through the woods, the way he had come in the early spring.

It was not an easy journey back. Whenever he thought of his partner, his steps faltered. He did not race, but took careful note of the land he was passing through once more. Perhaps he would return next year. He thought of Tesh and Tash. They would be missing him. So would everyone. He thought of his house, so lovingly built. When he thought of the village, his steps lightened and he moved faster. The words of the Great Being kept coming back: 'The people need you. Woods up to here will go - bring to safety - be very careful' So he went, different thoughts alternating in his head. He hunted roots and grubs, found wood rabbits, fed well. But he was careful. He went like a shadow through the woods. Nothing noticed him.

Coming nearer the village, he knew that something was wrong. It was like a huge dark cloud ahead. The trees were wrong. They were hurting. Later, the hurt became painful. Later still, the faintest trace of smoke was in the air. Had there been a fire? It was dry weather but people should be safe at the edge of the woods.

There was fear ahead. Fear, anger and much unhappiness. A huge confused feeling. He tried to single Tesh out of the mass of energy. She was most in tune with him of all.

<Tesh,> he sent, <Thumpus. Coming back.>

Tesh was with the goats. They were disturbed and uneasy, as they had been ever since the men came. They were hard to milk now. They kicked at the bucket, and tended to send droppings into the milk if you weren't very careful and whipped it away. Other children were milking too. Minesh was with them, sharpened stick in her hand. With all the uproar in the woods there was no game to hunt anyway.

Suddenly, Tesh heard her name. She looked around, before she realised it was inside. Thumpus! It could only be Thumpus. Her heart leapt. Her concentration lapsed and the goat kicked viciously, sending the bucket spinning away. Tesh sprang back. Luckily, she had only just started milking. She retrieved the bucket.

'Minesh!' Minesh walked over. 'It's Thumpus. He's back. On his way, at least. Please take over milking. I want to try to contact him. He's still far away and it needs concentration.'

Minesh took the bucket immediately.

'He mustn't come into this - they'd spear him or something.'

Tesh concentrated. <Thumpus. Take care. Danger. Many people.>

Instantly there was a reply:

<Tesh,> softly, lovingly. Then, 'What wrong? Bad feeling.>

<Strangers have come. Cutting down woods. Soldiers.> Thumpus wouldn't know what a soldier was so she sent an image of the men on horseback carrying swords.

<Be there tonight.>

<Be careful. Don't come daytime. After dark. Be *very* careful.>

The news spread instantly among the people. They agreed to meet after dark to welcome Thumpus back. Suresh was doubtful that Thumpus should come back. He left his hives and tramped far into the woods, beyond the already advancing line where the trees were being felled, out to the clearing where he and Thumpus had marked the nests last year. Then he sent thoughts out to Thumpus:

<Thumpus - Suresh. Hear me? In bees' nest clearing.>

<Can hear. Coming. Soon there.>

Suresh sat on a log and waited. Normally, he would have checked the bees' nests around, but he was deeply disturbed. He felt that Thumpus' return was bringing everything to a head. Even here, the air smelt quite strongly of smoke from the burning brushwood nearer the village. He sighed and settled down to wait.

It was more than an hour before Thumpus arrived in the clearing, cautiously sensing around before approaching Suresh. He was much thinner, and his hair was very matted, giving him a wild appearance. Suresh grinned with pleasure. There had been a lot more joy in his life, a lot more happiness, since he knew Thumpus, a happiness which was now threatened as the world he had left began to catch up with him.

<What is?> asked Thumpus. <Terrible bad feeling from trees. Smoke smell in air. Bad energy direction village. Nasty dreams.> He couldn't bring himself to send about the experience with the Great Being. Not yet. It would mean too much explanation.

But Suresh would not be hurried.

<Good journey?> he queried. <Find mate?>

<Long but good. Mate gone away for cubbing.> Thumpus glanced in the direction of the white peaks which had loomed over their mating. They sat for a moment, savouring renewed friendship, Suresh tickling the shaggy beast's neck.

<Huge changes in village. Many men come. Cut trees. Other men force them. Plan to cut all forest. Violence, burn-

ing. Like my childhood again.> Thumpus turned his head and looked at Suresh with his big, yellow-brown eyes. Suresh felt calmer. What a wonderful animal this was.

<Think all must leave or children taken away. But where?> Suresh paused. The only direction was the forest, but they knew little about it, and were a very vulnerable group. Thumpus remembered the images from his mate of her land, quiet and relatively peaceful, much like *his* woods had been. He remembered the message the Great Being had given. And knew what he had to do.

<Thumpus guide to mate's land. But long, long journey.>

Suresh looked at him, long and slow, but said nothing. Finally, holding back tears, he responded:

<Come after dark so forest-killers not see. People all know, will wait - Tesh, Tash. Take great care.>

They went together back towards the village, each with a heavy heart. Thumpus wanted to get closer, to sense better what was happening. Finally, as Suresh turned to avoid the main centre of the tree felling, Thumpus left him, continuing directly towards the noise of cutting and crashing timber. Suresh knew he would be careful. The warning had been given.

As Thumpus approached the noise, he began to feel more and more depressed. The feeling came from the trees themselves - in some rudimentary sense they were aware of their impending doom and that of their fellows. But it also felt as if part of *him* was dying. Perhaps he *had* been a guardian of the forest as his mate had told him. He had never been conscious of it until now, when it seemed to be too late. Was his job to lead the people away from the sylvan carnage to a place where even he had never been? Could he do it? Could *they* do it? It would have to be soon, or they would never get through by winter.

He moved parallel to the edge of the felling area, an unnoticed shadow. It was all very systematic. Where he was standing, the trees had been marked with red dots. As he came to the end of the felling area, another line of red dots extended through the forest, and one went back towards the noise of crashing and sawing. They were cutting in blocks. He padded along the line beyond the area of cut. It seemed to go on forever. He came to another line of dots heading back towards the forest edge - the second block, not yet worked. After a while he found a third block marked. He returned to the scene of devastation. It was like an ants' nest! Some men were chopping and sawing. Others were cutting off branches. Teams of huge animals were straining to pull stripped tree trunks back towards the village. Large fires were burning underbrush and branches.

Thumpus panted heavily. He wanted to howl in misery, but dared not, for fear of drawing attention to himself. Eventually, he retreated to the bees' glade, a place less affected by the carnage. He had planned to announce his return with some glorious thumps to let everyone know he was back. Now he had never felt less like thumping in his life. His tail twitched idly. He found some grubs in a rotten log and ate them. Perhaps the people would give him potatoes when he returned tonight. He was really hungry. He sent to Tesh and Tash:

<Potatoes? Hungry tonight.> But there was no answer. Thumpus dozed, head on paws as the long evening drew in. It was light till late at this time of the year.

When dusk fell, he worked his way along the edge of the now quiet cut area. The great, sprawling camp which housed the workers was to the west side of the village, like a boil on the landscape. The village itself had been left alone - for the time being - waiting for the Grand Duke to send word on its future. The grey-haired commander had declared it strictly out of bounds after things had been stolen early on. Guards were on duty to stop people from the camp entering.

Thumpus worked his way across to the east. He was very careful, but it was quiet. Camp fires lit up the sky - there was no shortage of wood.

<Coming in,> sent Thumpus and this time Tesh and Tash returned his message:

<Very happy! But take care.>

Thumpus reached the village without incident. Everyone was there, around a fire outside Prush and Lelesh's. It was a small fire in contrast to the profligacy in the nearby camp. The night was quiet. Between the houses, all was as it had been. The people gathered round him, Tesh and Tash in the forefront, hugging his neck, the other children close behind. His hut had fresh straw. For a moment, everyone was happy again.

Smiling, Lelesh brought out a big steaming pot. 'We thought you might like potatoes,' she said.

The Chronicles of Thumpus Wumpus

15.

Thumpus captured!

Thumpus shared his experiences very briefly, through Tesh. He did not share anything about the Great Being's message, only that he had found a mate after a long journey, hard for both of them.

'She is a sort of custodian of the woods in her region. She sends that it is a good place, something like this *was*,' Tesh translated.

Then it was Indalesh's turn to speak for the group. Although she could pick up some of Thumpus' thoughts, she couldn't send, so Tesh, who was becoming the 'official translator' passed the images to Thumpus.

<More and more people are coming every day. They seem to intend to cut all the woods down, section by section. Our lives are ruined. Only the soldiers stop them from plundering the village. They have said they will take the children away downhill to where the big towns are. We believe we must move from here, and soon, but where should we go? Down the hill everything is more or less like it is becoming here, Suresh says. If we go along the forest edge, the destruction will soon catch up with us. The only way is into the woods but that is completely unknown territory and we would have to go far, far away to escape this.>

After she had spoken, everyone was silent for a time. They had discussed the problem endlessly together and could see no other solution except moving on. The life being demonstrated before them was hateful. In spite of the soldiers' protection, their fields were trampled, their stock of goats diminishing. Thumpus also felt there was no alternative. He couldn't even make a homecoming wump for fear of attracting attention, and he would never be able to stay in the little group of houses in the daytime again.

<Will lead,> he sent, <to mate's land. Long journey. Must go soon or no time before winter.>

Tash and Tesh jumped for joy - an adventure! Indalesh and Suresh looked grim. They had picked up the implication about the length of the journey. It was only June now! Tesh finally remembered to translate for the others. The result was the same - the young ones were excited, the adults worried. What would they take? How would they carry things? There were no roads, or even paths.

<Summer can live off woods. Early autumn can live off woods. Not winter. Must get there by winter,> Thumpus sent.

Minesh and Tansh nodded. They had been learning about weapons from the soldiers. One of the off-duty soldiers was nice enough and had shown them how to make and shoot bows and arrows. They had no metal, but hard, sharpened hazel sticks were almost as good. The forest would provide medicine and food - most of the women were good with woodland plants and herbs, the mushroom season was coming round again, and Suresh was the bee expert. Thumpus would keep them out of danger. Perhaps they could do it. Each person would carry a bundle of their most essential things.

They all agreed that Indalesh would tell the commander that they had decided to go down the hill and resettle in the towns there. That would please him - they were no longer welcome in their own place anyway. Then they would leave before dawn, going in a downhill direction. That way it was less likely they would be followed.

A week was the minimum time needed to sort everything out. The goats would have to be left behind. All the food that would last a little would be prepared so they would have something to start off with. Their lifestyle had made them strong and hardy. Even Indalesh could still walk well if she had to. The flame of hope flickered.

It was late when they left the fire circle. Thumpus would stay in his house and leave before first light - not so long away. Tesh and Tash could hardly bear to be parted from him, but eventually went indoors.

At the edge of the village a shadowy figure moved away - a sentinel posted by the commander. He hadn't been able to hear what they had said, but he had seen the strange animal in their midst, apparently talking with them. Thumpus, sleepy and preoccupied, didn't notice him at all.

'It was an animal, sir, about as big as a small cow. All shaggy hair and long ears. Brown, I think, but it was hard to see in the firelight. They were with it all evening, not at all afraid of it. They seemed to be talking with it. I wasn't close enough to hear what they said.'

'Don't be ridiculous, man. Animals don't talk. You woke me for this? Have you been dreaming? If so ...'

'No, sir. It was true. I can't say for sure that they were talking. They seemed to be. But the animal was there all right. It was by that empty hut in the centre. It seemed like everyone was there. They must have been talking with it.'

'A talking animal! Maybe they have found some curiosity of the woods. The Grand Duke would be interested in that! Well done, man. We'll investigate in the morning.'

By 7 o'clock the commander was in the village, with two soldiers. Thumpus had departed, but there was clear evidence that something had been lying in the hut. There was an impression in the straw and a fire had been burning the night before. And the villagers were sleeping exceptionally late -

usually everyone was about by now. The commander left. He, himself, would watch that night.

That day, Indalesh went to him and said that the villagers planned to go down the hill in a week - life was rough with the loggers nearby, she explained, it would be better in the settled country. The commander had no objections. One of his main challenges had been to keep camp and village apart.

The village was back to its normal hours. In the late evening, when Thumpus arrived, the only welcoming party was Tesh and Tash, who would not be put to bed, and Prush and Lelesh with more potatoes. The harvest had been reasonable last year and they had stored well. A tiny fire was lit as a symbol. Thumpus was not in a very good mood. He had decided to try to fatten up for the long journey ahead, but all the small animals seemed to have evacuated the area - the woods were dead already! So it was roots and grubs again. The potatoes cheered him up somewhat, but Tash and Tesh were under strict orders not to stay up late, so, after many cuddles and protestations of love, they left him.

'It's no fun now,' thought Thumpus, who was wakeful. 'In the day, when everyone's here, I can't come. Now, when I want company, no-one else is here.' He snuggled down in the straw of his house and went to sleep anyway.

The commander had been watching the little scene. They seemed to be feeding the animal a huge pot of potatoes. Astonished, he crept quietly away to his soldiers, who had kept back for fear of discovery. The Grand Duke would certainly be pleased to have this one in his menagerie. The only thing was, how to catch it? It was certainly quite big, but it seemed gentle enough. Still, he would take no chances. The only plan he could think of which might succeed was to build a cage on a cart. Then, when the village was asleep, a group of soldiers, well armed with sharp spears, would creep up on the hut where the beast slept and surround the entrance. They would have to hold him trapped there till the cart arrived, with more soldiers.

All of this would wake the village, and the villagers would have to be held back till the animal could be prodded with spears up a ramp and into the cage, which could then be closed.

To prepare everything and train the soldiers would take a little time. The commander decided that the operation would take place not next night, but the one after. Next morning, he selected a band of his best men and some carpenters, swore them to the strictest secrecy and told them that he wanted the special animal captured for the zoo at the main city, Gunje. He didn't tell them about his plan to give it to the Grand Duke. There was no love lost for himand one of the soldiers might have decided to spear the beast out of spite.

The next day, preparations began. Strong wooden beams and staves built a cage on one of the carts. The soldiers were taken well away from the area and drilled. That night there was a practice exercise on the other side of the camp, with a plan of the village marked out on a clear piece of ground, pegs driven into the earth showing the corners of the houses. Small fires lit the area dimly.

The soldiers rehearsed again and again till the commander thought they would be able to approach the village quietly. He was a thorough man but, finally, even he was satisfied that everything was as good as it could be. Stealth was of the essence. If the beast woke up and ran away before they could corner it in its hut, they would never catch it. No-one had caught the slightest glimpse or sound of it during the day. As a reward for their diligence, the soldiers were given permission to sleep late. Next afternoon the plan was rehearsed again in the light.

Thumpus arrived as usual, just after dark, evading observation with ease. He was becoming blasé about the situation. As far as he could tell, the villagers seemed to be left alone by the incomers. And it was only three days till the departure. He told himself he came in each night to give support to the people, but he enjoyed the potato suppers very much and it was pleasant to be with Tesh and Tash, even for a little while. Soon they'd all be together again on the march. After he had thoroughly stuffed himself and the children had gone to bed, he cuddled into his straw and fell into a deep sleep.

Sometime in the early hours he began to twitch restlessly with bad dreams. Two enormous bears had cornered him and were closing on him relentlessly. He whined in his sleep. A dozen soldiers, silently creeping up on the hut, paused, then came on. Finally, they encircled the hut. The commander, waiting behind, nodded. Part one according to plan! He lifted a cloth from a tiny lamp, the signal for the cart to come from the camp. Now the noise would begin.

The bears snarled at Thumpus, their teeth sharp and white. There was nothing he could do - he cringed back and shivered. Suddenly he was wide awake. People smell. Fear. He poked his head out into the faint moonlight. A ring of spears rose and glinted. He was cornered by the soldiers! And there was no way out. He panicked, gave a howl to wake the dead and sent a desperate telepathic message:

<Help! Soldiers!>

More soldiers ran into the village, surrounding the area. Tesh and Tash were down in a flash, in their night-clothes. They had also had a disturbed sleep. Prush and Lelesh followed. All over the village people jumped up. They were being invaded! Suresh came running. But it was too late. A ring of steel spears held them off, as it held Thumpus penned. The cart creaked and groaned as it drew up to the scene, horses whinnying as they smelt Thumpus. Lanterns were unveiled. The cart was turned and pulled back, its ramp dropped just behind the soldiers guarding Thumpus. It was surrounded by more soldiers.

'Make an opening to the ramp,' the commander ordered. Now Thumpus could leave the hut, but only up into the cage. Every other way was protected by spears. Soldiers began pounding on the back of the hut with a heavy bar. Soon the boards would shatter. There was no escape.

Thumpus' strongest method of defence was deception but, cornered like this against overwhelming odds, he cringed. The men did not seem to want to kill him. If he went up into the cart, at least he would still be alive. Slowly, tail at the ready as a last defence, he emerged from the hut. Some of the soldiers gasped. No-one had seen anything like it before. Despairingly, he climbed the ramp and entered the cage. Soldiers slammed the door shut and a big wooden bar was placed across it. Thumpus' magnificent tail hung through the bars. He didn't even have room to swing it.

'Retreat!' ordered the commander. Forming a phalanx around the cart, the soldiers began to withdraw. It had all taken less than ten minutes. 'Meticulous,' thought the commander to himself, well pleased.

Indalesh, who had struggled into her clothes, pushed into the stunned crowd. As she took in the horror of what was going on, she found her voice.

'That animal is ours. Release him immediately!' she shouted at the commander, whose back was already half-turned. He looked back again at the villager.

'This animal is confiscated for the pleasure of the Grand Duke,' he said pompously. 'Now, return to your houses and sleep. No-one is to be out of doors.' But Tash, Tesh and Suresh were already away.

Despair took hold of the villagers. Their Thumpus had been taken; everyone felt his anguish and misery. Their *guide* had been taken; without him, how could they ever reach the faraway land where they hoped to rebuild their community in safety? Utterly dejected, the people returned to their houses.

'Meeting. First thing in the morning,' was all Indalesh could make herself say.

The Chronicles of Thumpus Wumpus

16.

Rescue

As Suresh ran out of his house he guessed immediately what was happening. Coming on the dreadful scene, he sent as strongly as he could to Tash and Tesh:

<Get coats and boots. Get out of back door and away. Meet at downhill/dawn edge of village. Follow cart.>

Poor Thumpus was so distraught he didn't get the message, but the children did. They didn't hesitate. It was too painful to watch Thumpus being captured. Here was something they could do. Only Prush noticed them running back to the house. She turned, but Indalesh laid a hand on her arm.

'Suresh has a plan,' she whispered. 'I heard. Don't draw attention to them.'

The trio met in no time at the prearranged spot, the children with coats over their arms and unlaced boots.

'Put your coats on and do up your boots,' said Suresh, 'then we'll follow the cart. It'll have to stop to organise things. Then they'll send it off downhill on the new track. We must keep up with it, but out of sight. Now let's move.'

Dark coats over night things and boots laced, the children followed Suresh, who had suddenly become a leader. As they moved, the soldiers fanned out round the village. But they were already through the cordon. They crept round to a slight rise to the east of the camp. There were still some scattered trees to give cover, and Suresh felt they were safe enough in the dark. The cart had stopped in the main camp, by fires which had suddenly sprung up. Thumpus could be seen dimly in the cage, tail feebly twitching.

'We've got to contact him,' whispered Suresh. 'Tesh, you try. You're the best connected of all of us.'

Tesh sent, as strongly as she could:

<Thumpus! Thumpus! Don't panic. We're here - Tesh, Tash and Suresh. We'll get you out somehow.>

But Thumpus had gone completely to pieces. He should never have come back to the village. How *could* he have been so careless? Dozens of soldiers, and he had been oblivious to the danger. He *deserved* to be taken. He was a useless, hopeless animal. Now the people would have no-one to guide them through the forest. He had let down the Great Being. He might as well die anyway. Somewhere at the edge of his awareness he heard Tesh's message, but he paid no attention to it. He had become a self-pitying wreck.

'He's not answering,' said Tesh miserably. Suresh looked at her. What could they do? - she was their best hope. Suddenly he remembered his own despair when he was taken from *his* village as a child.

'I think he's so miserable, he won't hear,' he said. 'I've an idea. See if you can *listen* to him, pick up his thoughts and answer them.'

Tesh, Tash and Suresh tuned in as tight as they could, trying to cut out the medley of inner noise from the soldiers and the camp. It was Tesh, as usual, who picked him out.

<Miserable, useless, hopeless rubbish, let everyone down. Deserve all I get! Thumpus no good.> Nudging the others to let them know she was in contact, she sent back:

<Brave, sensitive, loving Thumpus, best of all Thumpii. Gorgeous one!>

There was a moment's silence, then:

<Who? Tesh? Oh help! - Where?>

Suresh had been right. She had got his attention. The others had picked it up easily. Thumpus had *sent*!

Suresh replied instantly. <Tesh, Tash, Suresh. On knoll, sunrise side of camp. Thumpus, don't worry! Get you out somehow. Cheer up. Sending you downhill. Will be guard. Listen to No. 1 man. Get thoughts. Then all make escape plan. We very close, follow unseen. Now will go a little ahead. Keep in touch.>

<Love you, Thumpus,> was all Tash sent. He was crying.

Thumpus' thought came back. <Love you all. Will try now. Keep aware.>

With the contact, the captured beast's depression began to lift. He started to observe his surroundings. One man, with a fancy uniform, was standing looking at him. This must be the No. 1 man! Thumpus tuned in.

The man was thinking, 'He seems docile enough. Still, one never knows. And people will mob the cart on the way down. Sergeant Jarensh and five men are all I can spare. I'll send them off now. They can take a rest a few kilometres down the road. They'll be away, before the villagers awake and start complaining.'

'Jarensh. Here!' Sergeant Jarensh sprang to attention. 'Take five men. You're in charge of a detail to take the animal to the Grand Duke's palace. Prepare night packs. Take a camp breakfast. I'll give you money for the journey. You can buy supplies and lodgings. You have 30 minutes.'

'Yessir.' The sergeant looked at the men, still massed around the cart, picked five and barked instructions. All ran off. The commander turned to the other soldiers.

'Remain on guard. You! Go get a message from the village contingent as to the state of things there.' He walked away to a tent, to write a note to the Vizier and to get the men their money.

<Dear friends,> Thumpus sent. <Got him. Six soldiers to take downhill. Will rest not far away. Then chance.>

<Heard you,> replied Suresh. <Clear as bell. Will go on a little. Keep away in tree cover. Stay in touch!>

In no time at all the soldiers were back. The commander returned from his tent, sealing an envelope.

'Jarensh! All here? Good. These are your instructions. You will keep this animal safe. Never open the door. Don't allow anyone to approach the cage closely. There is money here to stay at inns on the journey - Special Privilege! Take good care of the horses. And Jarensh, this animal is a gift for the Grand Duke. To be delivered to the Vizier in good condition. Feed it water and boiled potatoes. Return here immediately with confirmation of delivery.

'When you get a decent way from the village, say after first light, stop. Have breakfast and a short rest at the roadside. Then move straight through the next villages. We don't know what contacts the people here have with them. We'll take any chances.'

'Yessir. Understood.'

'Good man!' One of the soldiers jumped up on the front of the cart, grabbed the reins and the vehicle moved forward with a jolt. Sergeant Jarensh jumped up beside him, the others lined up on either side of the cart, and the party moved out of the firelight. The commander turned to the rest of his men.

'Well done, men. At ease and stand down!'

Thumpus sent, <On way.>

In the dark and on the very rough track the soldiers could only go at a slow walking pace. The jolting of the unsprung cart was dreadful for Thumpus, but Suresh suggested that he examine the thoughts of the soldiers, to get ideas for an escape plan. This concentrated his mind a little.

It was no problem for the rescue party to keep up with the slow pace of the soldiers and in the dim, waning moonlight there was little chance of being spotted. But noise could bea problem, so the three villagers kept well away to the left and tried to avoid treading on sticks. They were all used to walking in woodland and this was grassland with trees rather than woodland proper, which made it easier. All the same, they took a lot of care.

<All sleepy,> came a message from Thumpus. <Resentful. Don't want animal go to 'Gran Dook'.>

<Encourage sleepiness,> sent Suresh. An idea was forming in his head. If, all together, they could send thoughts of deep sleep they might make the soldiers sleep so deeply that they could creep up, free Thumpus and be far away before anyone woke. He did not speak, but the others picked up the plan and agreed. Thumpus began to concentrate on Sergeant Jarensh, who was getting hungry as well as sleepy.

'Right, lads,' said Jarensh as first light touched the sky. 'We're about 6k away now, enough to have some breakfast and a short snooze. Pull the cart off at the next flat bit, Ronsh.'

In a minute or two Ronsh spotted a good place and obliged. They unhitched the horses and tethered them to a nearby tree, with some hay.

'Aw, that's better. What a blooming job! Guarding some queer animal to send to the GD. There'll be people gawping all down the road. First, Commander said it was for the zoo. Now it's for the blankety Duke himself.'

'At least we'll get a proper bed at night,' chipped in one of the others. 'I feel like I could sleep for days.'

'Don't be too sure,' said Jarensh. 'We'll have to keep a watch over this thing,' - he gestured at Thumpus, apparently dozing in the cart - 'or some wag'll let him loose in a town and there'll be hell to pay. Anyway, there's good sausage and black bread for breakfast and we can take a snooze for an hour or so. All but one of us!' he added.

They spread themselves around on the bank by the cart and lay back. Jarensh opened the pack from the cook, and laid a plentiful breakfast before them. Thumpus simply magnified their own thoughts back to them: <Eat, then sleep.> The others crept silently to within about 50 metres. Breakfast smells wafted over to them. Thumpus drooled at the food.

While the soldiers, supported by the thoughts of the watchers, finished off every crumb of the breakfast, Suresh sent his friends the plan.

<They'll set a guard. Must all together try and think him to sleep. Thumpus, send calm, deep sleep thoughts; Tesh, send calm thoughts to horses while Tash and I move bar and swing door back. Then we're away, quiet as mice, still sending calm, deep sleep thoughts.> Everyone assented. It was their best chance.

'Definitely time for a doze, lads,' said the sergeant. He glanced around. Some of the others were already taking one. 'Buresh, you keep watch. The animal looks quiet enough, but we'll take no chances. Wake us in an hour.'

Buresh groaned, but propped himself up on his coat and prepared to keep watch. Within a couple of minutes everybody else was well asleep.

'Stupid,' thought Buresh. 'There's nothing to watch for. Damn the Grand Duke! So peaceful, quiet, so sleepy - just lie back a moment ...' ... He was away.

Thumpus released his concentration for a second to send, <All sleeping.>

'Right,' breathed Suresh aloud, 'let's go!'

Silently they crept down to the cart. There was plenty of light now, though the sun had not yet risen. Tesh concentrated on the horses, but Thumpus had done such a magnificent job that even they seemed to be dozing. Their eyes were shut.

Tash and Suresh climbed on the back of the cart as quietly as they could. It creaked slightly, but no-one stirred. Very carefully, Suresh began to work at the bar. Tash pushed the door in a little so it would move more easily. It was stiff, but slowly they managed to slide it back, bit by bit. Tiny squeaks from the bar sounded like sirens in their ears but still nobody woke. Finally, the bar came out. Suresh laid it carefully along the side of the cart. Now they could open the door!

Suresh lifted it slightly to stop it creaking. It was heavy. Then they saw they'd forgotten a simple thing. With the back of the cart up, the door would only open a few centimetres. Thumpus pushed his head through. It wouldn't go. Tash and Suresh had to climb down from the cart and undo the back flap, held by two metal pins. It was even stiffer and they had to work the pins out. They squeaked quite loudly. Someone stirred, moaned. They froze still. Thumpus paid no more attention to the exit, concentrating once more on calmness, sleep.

At last, the rear flap was down. From far away down the hill, there was noise - the first morning supply cart! They swung the door open, slowly, slowly. Thumpus' head came through, his shoulders - he was out, springing lightly to the ground. Tash turned to follow, but Suresh sent, <Wait! Shut.> They pushed the door back and replaced the bar so it wouldn't swing. Then they, too, were down. Tesh, who had been sending sleepy thoughts to the horses, was dozing herself. They roused her, fingers on lips, still sending, <Sleep, calm,> as they moved off in the direction of the village.

A few minutes later, the supply cart trundled noisily up the slope.

'Strange,' thought the carter, as he saw the sleeping soldiers beside their empty cart. 'Still,' he thought, 'None of my business!' The group slept on.

Tesh, Tash and Suresh were feeling very tired, not just from sending sleep thoughts to the soldiers but because they, themselves, had had no sleep. But there was no time to wait. Sooner or later the soldiers would wake up, perhaps when the cart they had heard went past. But Thumpus was very lively and hungry after his imprisonment. Despite their fatigue, everybody's spirits were high - Thumpus was free again!

They moved fast through the semi-open land, angling away from the track. Tash hitched a ride on Thumpus' back. It seemed too dangerous to approach the village in broad daylight, so they took a roundabout route to bring them to the forest edge farther to the east. There they stopped for a moment.

'Somehow we must let them know,' said Suresh as they leant against trees for support, panting.

'Indalesh,' said Tesh. 'She's learnt to receive a bit. Perhaps if we all send the same thought to her it will be strong enough for her to pick up.'

They agreed to send the simplest message: <Thumpus free. All OK. In forest. Must leave. Come *now*!>

They had never tried sending a specific message as a group before. Tash counted, 'One, two, three -' and they all sent to Indalesh together. At first, the message was just a babble, as everyone sent at a different speed, so they worked out a rhythm. The second time was much better and the third, clear and deafening. Suresh was suddenly worried that one of the workers at the camp might have the ability and receive it too, though it seemed unlikely.

Indalesh was sitting outside her house, thinking. She was concerned, particularly for Prush and Lelesh. She had some confidence in Suresh; he had changed greatly, especially in the last few months. She hoped the three rescuers could work out a plan. She was sure they could communicate with Thumpus without the soldiers knowing. But Prush and Lelesh were beside themselves with anxiety. Young children and soldiers didn't mix. Lelesh was blaming herself. Why hadn't she stopped them in those terrible moments when all were mesmerised by the capture of Thumpus?

The day had dawned; the camp machines were starting up their dreadful din and the workers were setting off for the day's destruction in the woods. There didn't seem to be any soldiers about. Maybe they were having a lie-in after their night's work. Everything seemed normal enough. She sighed. She wanted to send to the rescuers, to ask them how it was going. But she knew she couldn't project her thoughts over long distances. Suddenly there was a loud, confused inner noise in her head, from the woods to the east of the village. She looked over that way, half-expecting to see someone. The inner noise came again. This time she had a picture of Thumpus. They were trying to send to her! If it was from the woods, they were probably all right. Suddenly a clear message in her head almost knocked her over, it was so loud.

<Thumpus free. All OK. In forest. Must leave. Come *now*!>

She looked around, sure that other people had heard. But normality reigned. She calmed herself.

<Received,> she sent back, as strongly as she could. Then, again and again, <Received.> She hoped they would hear it. She was useless at sending.

<Sent: received,> relayed Thumpus to his friends. <Not clear, but pretty sure.>

Thumpus was by far the strongest sender and receiver. Suresh hoped he was right. Every moment he was waiting for the alarm to sound in the camp. Making his voice sound confident, he said, 'Good. Now we must move on. Any time the alarm may sound. We'll go to the bees' place. Then you can rest.'

The children were exhausted and hungry but determined not to give in. It was two hours' walk.

'Can you give Tesh a ride, Thumpus?'

Tesh protested, but Suresh was firm. After an hour, Tesh, who had dozed on Thumpus' rocking back, swapped with Tash, who was staggering, hand held by Suresh. When they finally arrived, there was a little stream to drink from. The children collapsed on a bank and were immediately asleep.

<Thumpus, look after the children. Find roots they can eat raw. Going back to see what's happening. Others don't know way here and if No.1 man finds out, he may try to stop them coming.>

Suresh was also very tired himself, but the drink had revived him somewhat and he was a tough fellow. 'It's not the first time I've missed a night's sleep,' he thought to himself as he trudged back through the woods.

Indalesh gathered the villagers together in a spot which couldn't be seen from the camp. Almost everyone was there children were sent to fetch those few who had stirred themselves early to be with goats and plantings.

Indalesh shared her news.

'Thumpus has escaped. They've all got into the forest over there. They want us to leave now. I propose we leave in one hour. I think you all have your things more or less ready, anyway.'

It was true. Although they had agreed on a week's preparation, everybody had put together their travelling pack the day after the decision to leave. It was not a hard thing to do. The hard thing was leaving the home where most of them had been born. But that home - the quiet, peaceful spot on the edge of the friendly forest - had been disrupted for ever. There was no alternative.

It was late morning when they left, 20 people in a bunch, silent, some shedding tears, the children in the middle. All were heavily laden with bundles or backpacks. They had found Suresh's pack already prepared - he had been working on it the evening before the soldiers arrived to trap Thumpus. Tansh carried it, hoping that everything was in it and that they would meet him soon - the double load was as much as he could stagger with. They left from the east side of the village, protected as far as possible from sight of the camp, and walked a long way through the scattered trees before they turned to the forest's edge. Prush and Lelesh carried Tash and Tesh's small packs as well as their own.

There was no sign from the camp that anyone had noticed them at all. But Suresh, arriving back at the edge of the woods, did see them and set a parallel course to meet them when they turned towards him.

'You were quicker than I could have believed.' He smiled, a rare event for Suresh. 'We are safe and about two hours' walk from here. There we can stop for a little, but we must go on till dark in case of pursuit. After that we will be safe, I think. Even if they've seen where we've gone, I don't think they'll bother to venture far into the woods. They'll be pleased enough to have our houses.'

With relief, Tansh handed him his pack. The little group of dispossessed villagers plodded away through the trees, led by Suresh.

At the camp, the commander indulged himself and his soldiers by lying in late. A good job, he reflected, well done. When he had breakfasted, he glanced over at the village. It was quiet, but smoke was rising from the chimneys as usual. If the villagers left, he would billet there, with some of the soldiers. Better than camping. He wondered how the troops guarding Thumpus were getting along. As he pulled on his uniform, he decided to review the remainder. A lie-in was one thing, but it could lead to sloppiness. A good parade would renew discipline.

As he called the troops out for examination, a supply cart pulled in. After parade, he would check with the driver, who should have passed the escort.

The soldiers were, as he expected, sloppy. He went around the ranks carefully, pointing out the faults in each one's presentation. When he finished, he had his remaining NCO, a lance corporal, give them a short drill, which was badly led and carried out. As a result, he gave everyone a good dressing-down before he sent them to their stations guarding the wood-cutting operations - which really meant watching for deserters. Most of the workers were less than enthusiastic about being so far from home. He had a critical word with the lance corporal, telling him to set a better example to his men. Then he turned to find the carter - who had had a quick turn-around and left. Well, no matter. It was out of his hands now.

Some time after that, the carter passed the sleeping soldiers and the standing cart again on his way downhill. Some folks had nothing to do with their time! So-called soldiers! It would make a good tale at the inn.

It was after lunchtime when Buresh awoke. He yawned and stretched, damp after so long on the ground. He was hungry again. Then he remembered he was supposed to be guarding the cart, sat up straight and thanked his lucky stars he was the first to wake. He glanced over to the cage and saw the door was shut. There was no sign of the animal, but it was probably lying down at the bottom, where he couldn't see it. He'd better wake the others - the sergeant first.

Then a thought came to him - this was a chance! They were all still sleeping soundly - perhaps he could get away. He hated being a soldier. With the two horses he could travel far. There was a spare saddle in the cart in case of emergencies. He got to his feet and went over to the cart. The saddle was there; the animal wasn't! Someone must have come while they were sleeping and let it out. That decided him. If Sergeant Jarensh woke up and found out he hadn't guarded the big beast, he would be for the chop, good and proper. Quietly, one eye on the sleeping soldiers, he grabbed the saddle and moved over to the quiet horses. They seemed sleepy too. Had everyone been bewitched? He unhitched the horses' reins, moving them off along the grass by the side of the track. He would put the saddle on down the road, out of sight and earshot ...

Sergeant Jarensh woke at about half-past two, feeling an inner pressure. He stumbled off to find a bush. As he returned, now more awake, he became aware that things were eerily quiet. What was Buresh doing? He glanced at the sun. Lord, it was late - they had slept for hours. Buresh would get it! He looked around. Where was Buresh? Where were the horses? Hell and damnation! - where was the animal? Looking down at the other four sleeping soldiers, he knew his world had just fallen apart. It would be a court martial for him and years in some ghastly jail. He sighed. It hadn't been a bad life as a sergeant. Silently, he hefted his pack and stepped away downhill. He would have to find a new identity and a new job in a faraway place. He could do it. He hadn't made it to sergeant for nothing ...

At four o'clock, as the soft afternoon was whiling away, Ronsh opened his eyes, feeling damp. He was so stiff he could hardly get up, but when he did, he woke the other three immediately.

'Cripes! Wake up! Janesh and Buresh've gone. So 'ave the 'orses. So's the animal! They've taken off and ditched us!'

The other men pulled themselves into consciousness.

'We ain't got no food! We ain't got no money!'

'We ain't got no sergeant neither. We're free men, mates. We can make it back down'ill 'n' start over. No more soldiering for me!'

Sharing out what little food remained in their packs, the ex-soldiers set off down the track. There were coppers enough between them for the next meal. For later, their weapons would sell for a good price.

The cart remained, empty and forlorn, by the side of the track.

The Chronicles of Thumpus Wumpus

17

The Trek begins

Everyone was tired and hungry when they finally arrived at the bees' clearing, but glad to see Thumpus and the children. Thumpus was in a very good mood after his escape. Tesh and Tash had slept and were somewhat restored. There didn't appear to be any sign of pursuit. Suresh could hardly believe their good fortune. But he didn't let them stop for long. He reckoned that if they could keep going till dark, there would be no further pursuit. The soldiers weren't used to the forest and their horses found it hard going in the trackless country; as far as they were concerned, the villagers weren't important anyway. Suresh hoped that, realising that Thumpus had got away, the commander would give up. He was not stupid. There would be no chance of catching Thumpus in the thick of the woods.

The full story of their escape had to wait. The people plodded on, led by Thumpus, who took the tired children on his back in turn. As the light shaded and soft summer clouds began to glow with sun fire, a small clearing provided the perfect camping place. Packs were dropped, aching legs stretched out and a good fire gave comfort and kept off the worst of the flies. There was water in a burn for drinking and soothing swollen feet.

After they had eaten, the story of Thumpus' rescue was told and embellished by Tesh and Tash, who found new energy in the telling. They leant against Thumpus, a perfect back rest. As they heard the story, people looked at Suresh with new respect. He had turned into the natural leader of the group. There was no need for votes or discussion when Suresh proposed that they travel on for the next day, but after that only on alternate days, hunting and gathering in between, conserving strength and provisions for whatever lay ahead. Thumpus agreed for the time being; there were places further on, where it would not do to stop.

For now, the weather was gentle and warm. Dried moss made a soft underlay for beds. Sleep came easy, that first night away from home.

Suresh's day-on/day off system worked very well. After a day's break, everyone looked forward to a day's journey. After a day's journey, all eagerly anticipated a day's rest and food-gathering. There was a lot of resistance to grubs, Thumpus' favourite diet, but, as long as you shut your eyes, fried grub tasted quite good. On the other hand, berries were getting ripe in some clearings, and everybody liked them. Edible herbs and roots were to be found and they were tasty, but you had to know what you were looking for. Tansh and Minesh caught a few small animals, but other people weren't very good at it. Thumpus could find enough to keep himself in very good shape, but although the villagers didn't have to use up their meagre supplies, they weren't accumulating any more either. Slowly but steadily they went forward through the forest.

Tesh was having a particularly good time. She was strong enough to do a full day's walk and, knowing that the next day would be rest time for the younger children, she could chivvy them on and keep their spirits up. She enjoyed hunting for food too. It felt really good to bring back something for the evening meal. In between, she found time to pester Thumpus to show her how to use her abilities to sense other presences around them. Tash also did well at this, but he didn't quite have Tesh's gift. Suresh kept his counsel, but they could feel he was honing his telepathic skills as well. Thumpus was still always the best. His senses of smell and hearing were exceptional, as was his awareness of thoughts in the vicinity. He would get the thought forms first, and soon after supplement them with tiny noises or smells that Tesh and Tash had no inkling were around them.

Thumpus was delighted to be with the people, to be on his way back to his mate and doing the job the Great Being had asked him to do. But in the back of his head were worries - about the pace they were making, the distance they had to travel and about areas ahead where big beasts lurked and wild rivers rushed down from the mountains.

'Enjoy the good time now,' he thought to himself. 'If the Great Being wants us to get through, there'll be support enough.'

Tesh kept asking about the Great Being. On that night at the village when she had translated Thumpus' story, she had been awed by the picture Thumpus had sent of the dragon half in this world, half in some other unknown, awesome existence. As they travelled up towards the base of the great white-topped mountains where the physical bit of him, at least, was supposed to live, she pictured herself meeting this dragon, shimmering half in and half out of its formidable form. She practised addressing it in her head.

'Your Grace,' she would begin, remembering the way the commander had referred to the Grand Duke, who seemed to be the equivalent 'High Being' from down the hill, 'I am most pleased to meet your excellent Worship and honour every word you may be willing to address to me, your humble servant.'

But what would the dragon say to her in return? She couldn't really think of anything that such an august Being would want to say to a country girl like her. So she continued with the sort of things she herself would say: 'I know I'm only a simple village lass, without great education, but I'm ever so willing to learn, because I want to help things improve in this world, so greedy people won't come and cut down our forest and try to catch our good friend Thumpus and make terrible smoke over the village so we can hardly see and our eyes smart.' She would pause once more, trying to frame a reply that didn't want to come.

One rest day, with the mountains considerably nearer, the forest thinner and the streams so torrential that they had trouble finding crossing places, Tesh was out looking for food, not far from their camping place. She had already been strong and fit before the journey began, but now she was tough and lithe as well, brown-skinned and shining-eyed. As the people walked, more a part of the woods than they had ever been, everyone was stronger and more alive. Even Indalesh sometimes seemed like a child again, untiring as she hobbled through the forest, shedding stiffness and old age like raindrops off leaves. Though the sun was hot, the rain was warm and storms were few. Nature was being kind to them.

Tesh stopped gathering from a patch of wild roots she had found and looked through the trees at the white mountains towering above, rocks piling on rocks till they merged in the snowy distance. Absorbed in the beauty of the place, she did not even think of the Great Being, but suddenly he was there with her: not some awesome thing, but a small dragon, about as high as she was, standing on its rear legs.

'Do you know where Thumpus gets his tail?' it said, grinning. 'Copied off me!' It had a magnificent green scaly tail, nothing like Thumpus' really, but equally large. 'Course, his is duller than mine.'

'You're the dragon!' said Tesh, all her prepared speeches forgotten. It seemed crazy to address this cheeky, human-sized dragon as 'Your Grace'.

'That I am. And I thought it was about time to come and meet Tesh, who hears without ears and sees without eyes, just like I do.'

'But - I thought you would be different - more - distant.'

'Oh, I can be as distant as you like!' Suddenly the Great Being was hardly more than a speck up the mountain.

'Come back! I don't want you to be far away.' The dragon was beside her again, grinning hard.

'Yes, it's nice to be close, isn't it?' Suddenly the dragon was next to her and she had the feeling that they were marching together through the woods, kilometre after kilometre, although it didn't take any time at all. Somehow they had gone right around the mountains and were coming to a big open space in the trees, to a place where the sun was strong. There was Thumpus - another, slightly smaller Thumpus by his side *and* an utterly adorable baby Thumpus. She knew that this was where they would stop and make a new home. But there were also people there, a group of dark-skinned people coming towards them.

'It's their place!' cried Tesh, completely absorbed in the vision. 'They won't let us stay here.'

'Yes they will.' The dragon smiled. 'They have plenty of land and you have things to learn from each other. Just remember to ask them *properly*. - So you can have visions as well? I thought you could.'

The dragon was still looking at her, but it was suddenly moving away, up towards the mountain, growing larger as it did so, till it was gigantic - a Dragon, not a dragon.

'Don't go,' pleaded Tesh. 'You're not at all like I imagined you.'

But the retreating dragon was merging into the hill - or was the hill merging into it?

'Help Thumpus.' The words echoed in her head. 'Both of you together can bring the people through the trial.'

Suddenly she was back in her little patch of roots, the sky was blue, the mountains white through the trees. Had she been dreaming? But there was definitely a mark on the grass, where something had stood in front of her. Tesh felt tremendously happy and with it, wise and responsible. The Great Being had come to her, trusted her and told her she was important for their journey. She gathered a few more roots and made her way through the trees to the camp. Her experience was too special to share with anyone, not even Thumpus.

The Chronicles of Thumpus Wumpus

18.

Tal and Til

Steadily the summer days passed and the people, guided by Thumpus, traversed the endless forest. They were nearing the place where he had met his mate. The big mountain rivers he had so much trouble crossing in spring were now sparkling burns; only the huge boulders in their beds indicated that they could show another face. The party toiled round the gorge. Nothing had bothered them so far - there was good hunting at this time of the year and a big group with fire were not to be troubled lightly. If he became aware of anything in the vicinity, Thumpus projected an exaggerated image of the size of the group.

One day, he led them to a clearing he remembered very well indeed. He stopped.

<Here met mate,> he sent. <At least halfway now.> It was a good spot, with plenty of roots and berries, and mountain hares in abundance - if you could catch them.

'Let's stop here a bit,' said Tash. Suresh and Indalesh consulted with Thumpus. Would this be a good place to take a couple of days' pause?

<Way beyond here new. Mate says rough, hard going. More animals. Summer passing. If stop here, travel every day after.> From now on, Thumpus would be relying on his sense of direction and on images of her journey sent by his mate during their time together.

<How about - one day walk plus next morning walk, then half day rest?> sent Suresh.

<Can try,> returned Thumpus. <Autumn rains soon. Must find place in time build houses for winter. Collect food.>

Everyone had been putting off the thought of winter - winter without goats, without food-stocked houses. Autumn was already beginning and they still had nearly half the distance to go. Tash thought of the journey back to the village from their encounter with Kamal. Thumpus looked at him.

<Not that way.>

They were high up now, the mountain sides steep above them. At night they huddled together against the cold. As the journey progressed, hare skins accumulated; several of the women had dried them and they were sewn together. Though they weren't properly cured - there was no salt to spare - they made good warm rugs to lie on. The cold seemed more intense from the earth below than from the sky above at this time of year.

The two-day pause was an opportunity to gather food. Some people thought of stopping altogether, but at such a height it would be very rough in winter. After the rest, they headed onward by the easiest route they could find; it was indeed rougher going. They had to make detours round gorges and avoid tangled masses of fallen trees. Gradually, they snaked round the side of the mountains, so that their bulk eventually stood between the people and the village they had left.

Thumpus was relieved. The forest here was healthier, more vibrant, not under threat. He could hardly believe that the loggers could cut all the way to the mountain, but from the state of the trees behind them, it seemed that it would one day be so - another reason for moving on. Tesh remembered what her dragon - she thought of it as 'hers' because it had been so friendly and approachable - had said about a 'trial' and was more uneasy. She worked constantly at improving her inner skills, trying to appreciate and interpret the slightest energy change in the woods around them. Her senses were becoming very sharp indeed.

It was she and not Thumpus, preoccupied with the idea of seeing his mate again, who sensed something different in the forest ahead. It was still some way in front of them, not approaching - something with the potential to be big and violent. She sent a sharp thought to Thumpus.

<Check ahead!>

Thumpus reluctantly came out of his reverie and listened for thoughts in the direction indicated.

He made a soft 'grrrh' sound, the equivalent of 'Whoops'.

<Don't know this one, but nasty. In our way.>

Tesh called the group to a halt.

'There's a problem ahead,' she said. 'Something large and violent. It's keeping very quiet, but we can feel its thoughts.'

'Can we make a detour around it?' asked Nashe. Tesh forwarded the question to Thumpus.

<Hard. If big, has large territory. We make noise, smell. If avoid, must go very long way, keep moving.>

<Can we deflect,> sent Suresh, <send it after game in other direction or something?>

<Not for long enough. Group come together. Tesh, Tash, Thumpus, Suresh go little ahead. Try find out.>

Minesh and Tansh were out hunting, behind and uphill. They would pick up the people's trail and return for the midday pause. Suresh proposed the people should wait for the hunters to rejoin them while the four who could read thoughts should go forward. Tash was not as good as the other three, but they didn't think of leaving him out, apart from Prush who objected mildly. Suresh pointed out that the four of them were now used to working together with thought, which was the people's best defence of all.

They did not have to go far. Just through the trees, away from the varied thoughts of the others, it was much easier to get in touch with what was ahead.

<Two. In separate places,> sent Tesh excitedly.

Thumpus looked at her. Again she had noticed something before him. And he had been concentrating this time.

<Yes. Good.>

Tesh was pleased. She could be even sharper than Thumpus now. A thought came to her. Could they act as if they were one unit? Instead of competing against each other, they could combine their sensitivity - become as one. Then they would double their awareness. She shared this idea with her friends.

<All four would have more power,> agreed Suresh.

<First Thumpus and me. Then you come in.> Tesh thought Suresh could do it. She was not so sure about Tash.

<How?> sent Thumpus.

Tesh was in charge now, trusting her intuition.

<I'll make myself open. You try to come in to me - as if we were one. See what happens.> Tesh tried to take down all the barriers between herself and the others. She thought of how much she loved them, of how much they meant to her, of all the adventures they had shared. No separation.

Thumpus searched for her thoughts. How beautiful she was, like a calm lake in the forest. He loved her so much. Suddenly there was no Thumpus, no Tesh, just a 'one being'.

'Suresh, come!' said Tesh softly. 'It's wonderful.' Suresh nodded and began to think their - its - thoughts. How special! Like the bees in the hive, different forms but one consciousness. He loved them very much. Tears rolled down his face. And then three was one!

'Tash!' Tash looked at them all. Their faces were radiant. He loved them all, but Thumpus was his special friend. Thumpus who never left him out, Thumpus who made him feel big and valued, even if his ability was not quite as strong as the others. He loved him so. And then there was no Tash any more, only a great, big beautiful oneness - four bodies but one mind. Somehow it was Tesh's, though it wasn't Tesh but four-in-one. This new Tesh/not Tesh felt out over the forest. In its multiple mind, it was so aware it could actually see what lay ahead.

Tal, the great tiger of the woods, lay in his lair, tail twitching. He was the largest, most ferocious animal of the whole forest and he knew it. Til, his mate, was in another lair, about 3 kilometres downhill. They didn't live together. Although she was pretty aggressive herself, Til found him too violent, too liable to strike out. Besides, Tal couldn't stand cubs. They irritated him and he was liable to go for them. One strike from his great paws or a bite from his jaws meant the end of a little cub. Til had cubs right now; if something threatened them she would fight to the death. So Tal kept to himself. He wasn't unhappy about it. It was the way tigers were.

His tail twitched again. He was beginning to get hungry and he had a vague sense of unease, as if he were being watched. In her lair, Til's tail was twitching too, though she was not hungry.

The inner watchers saw it all - the two tigers, the three cubs, the lairs, the savagery of the great beasts up ahead. It made Kamal seem like a pet.

'I'm me,' thought Tash. 'It's wonderful to be one, but a bit scary, almost as scary as those animals. Besides, if we're one, they can't be my friends.' For a moment, there was him and one other. Then it fell apart and there were four of them again.

'You left,' said Tesh. 'How?'

'I was one, but I wasn't,' said Tash, confused. 'There was the thought 'I'm me' and then I was separate. For a moment you were still one, then it fell apart as well and you were three again.'

'So when we want to come apart, all we have to do is to think the thought 'I'm me',' said Suresh, grinning. 'You seem to have solved a problem we never thought of at the beginning - how to get out of it again.'

Thumpus licked Tash fondly. Tash swelled with pride. He might not be all that good at thought-sending, but he had joined with them, and made an important discovery too. Tesh didn't say anything. She seemed just the tiniest little touch jealous at his inadvertent discovery.

'Yes, that's the way,' he said, importantly. Suresh picked him up and threw him in the air.

'Well done!' he said.

They were all excited and somewhat overwhelmed at the power of what Tesh had led them into. It was as if they could see through the eyes of things in the forest at a distance.

On returning to the others, they found Minesh and Tansh with the others, anxiously fingering their hunting weapons.

'They won't be much use against what we have in front of us,' said Suresh. 'Two large and extremely ferocious forest animals, male and female, with cubs, hunting separately. I don't think we can fight them. Some of us, certainly, would die.'

<Have to go long, long way round,> sent Thumpus. <But - maybe more animals, farther away?>

Tesh was thinking hard.

'They have strength, but we have something new,' she told the group, explaining what had happened in the woods and how they had 'seen' the tigers. There were gasps from the others.

'Wonderful!' said Indalesh. 'We can certainly know exactly where they are and what they intend to do. But it doesn't stop them.'

'I have an idea,' continued Tesh. 'I think we may be able to pull other people into this unity we have found. Even if they aren't thought-readers. Alesh, will you let us try?' She chose Alesh because she was a stolid woman, the last person you would imagine to be telepathic. If they could do it with her, they could do it with anyone - or anything.

'Of course,' replied Alesh, smiling. 'But you'll not get me reading thoughts. I've tried and tried.'

'Go on, Mum,' said Jashe and Potish. 'You can do it!'

'Well, I'll give it another go.'

'This is a bit different,' said Suresh. He thought he understood what Tesh had in mind. It frightened him, but he was at least prepared to explore it.

Tesh stood slightly forward. Prush and Lelesh felt proud of her, not so much because she was a thought-reader, but because she *dared* and could take the lead.

As she had done before, Tesh opened herself. The others joined her - and they were one. It was easier this time. 'They' - the four-in-one - took a moment to check the tigers. Tal was getting hungrier. He was about to move out of his lair. Then they concentrated on Alesh. Each of them could see her clearly. It was strange: an inner and outer vision. Although Alesh was stolid outside, they could perceive inside and feeling inadequate. They felt their love for her, surrounding her with their loving thought - There was an involuntary 'Ooh!' and Alesh became one with them. The five of them, led by Tesh's consciousness, walked away through the trees, Alesh doing just as the others thought. Then they returned.

'I'm me,' thought Tash. As before, they quickly became separate.

'That was completely incredible!' shared the startled Alesh. 'I feel as if I've changed. As if a block has gone. I'm sure I could read thoughts now.'

<No time!> sent Thumpus hastily. <Tal coming this way. Til too!>

As Tal moved up and across the hillside to hunt, he gave a roar; Til stretched and followed. She wasn't terribly hungry, but after her mate had killed and eaten his fill, there would be some over for her. He was a good hunter. The cubs stayed, as they had learnt, in the shelter of the den. They were still small and vulnerable.

'We'll love them and enter them.' Tesh explained her idea. 'Then they will be peaceful and we can pass by without hurt.' Everyone gasped.

'Try it now,' urged Suresh, 'before they get too near.'

They made their unity again, located Tal and did as they had done with Alesh, surrounding him with love. It was hard to love such a violent beast, but in a terrible way, he was beautiful. Suddenly there was oneness - but not quite. It was as if Tesh's will to peace was being contested by a great hunger, and a powerful, exciting aggressiveness. Tal stopped dead and whined.

'I'm me,' thought Tash, and the group separated.

'Lord, that was powerful!' said Suresh.

<Must get him fed, first,> sent Thumpus, who, being an animal and having lived years in the woods, knew how other animals worked. <She not so hungry,> he added. He searched, inwardly. Tal was heading in their direction, though he didn't know they were there. A little off to the left, there were deer.

'Don't like this, but must do it,' thought Thumpus. 'Great Being, forgive me.' He just sent out the thought, <Food, right!>

Tal turned. In another few moments he had smelt the deer. 'Surely he would have anyway,' thought Thumpus, to comfort himself. Though he caught and ate small forest creatures, he did not like the idea of luring bigger deer to their death. Still, that was the way of tigers and deer.

<He kill now,> sent Thumpus. <In short time we go. Easy.>

Tal succeeded in catching one of the deer and proceeded to make a meal of what he considered to be the choicest bits. Til waited patiently nearby. The villagers started forward in a tight bunch, children at the centre. Everyone was armed with makeshift weapons - their last line of defence in case the risky plan did not succeed.

'Tash,' said Suresh. 'We need someone to be separate from the "unity" who can be aware of anything else that might be around and to warn the others if anything is going wrong. Would you do that for us?'

'Is it because I come out first?'

'Partly.' Suresh had not wanted to admit this. 'But it's an essential job,'. 'If we stopped too quickly, the beasts could still turn on us. All our attention has to be on peace and love. Someone must keep a watch around.'

Tash was glad to accept the explanation. It really was scary, joining with the consciousness of those ferocious beasts - two this time. And someone did need to look around, didn't they? He didn't question that too hard.

Hearts in mouths, the people moved forward. As they neared the spot, about 100 metres to the left, where Tal was lazily watching Til nibble at the kill, Thumpus, Tesh and Suresh went into unity and embraced the huge tigers in love. Thumpus had been right. While still ferocious and capable of attack, the tigers were much easier to engage with now.

<Special animals passing through,> the leader of the oneness presented. <Friendly, nice, no harm to tigers, soon leave territory.> The two tigers looked up, and in a moment heard the noise of the party passing through the forest so near them. Curious, they moved towards the sound.

'There they are!' whispered Prush. Hands gripped tight as the two huge yellow and black forms became visible through the trees, almost a part of the light and shade dappling the ground. 'Lord, they're beautiful.'

<Animals passing through, no harm. Don't bother them.> There was not much difficulty in controlling the beasts' urge to attack, but their curiosity was very strong. The tigers

walked close to the group, parallel to it, recording the different smells. They sensed the humans' fear.

<Special animals frightened. We are so big and powerful. No need to attack. No threat.> Lazily, Til lifted her head and gave a rolling growl. Everyone trembled.

'She's calling her cubs,' whispered Tash to the others, his role vindicated. 'I don't think we have to worry.'

In a few minutes, the tumbly little cubs came trotting through the forest, rushing up to their mother at the sight of the strangers. She licked them, keeping pace with the moving party.

<Together through territory.> The merged consciousness of animals and humans seemed to create one physical group. The tigers walked along as if mesmerised. But after a while the cubs fell behind. Til's instinct was stronger than the curiosity. She stopped with them. For a moment the unity wavered as she dropped out, pulled by something stronger than the inner bond. But then it re-established itself. Tal, the epitome of supreme physicality, continued to keep pace. The strange walk through the forest went on for one hour, then two. Some of the people were becoming tired. But the unity was not tired. The tiger had enough energy for all of them together and they were one with it. The younger children complained, but no-one dared to stop. It was lunchtime, but everyone kept on.

The ground started to drop away, the trees were thicker. There was a small river ahead.

The thought, <Edge of den territory,> came into the awareness of the unity. The group had reached the boundary of the inner, most protected part of the tiger's range.

<Special animals go on and away, no harm. Time to return to mate now.> Tesh, leader of one inner being, felt it was time to take the risk to separate the tiger physically from the group. Tal stopped, tail twitching. He gave an enormous roar that sent children clinging to their parents, then he turned and stalked away, almost instantly out of sight through the trees.

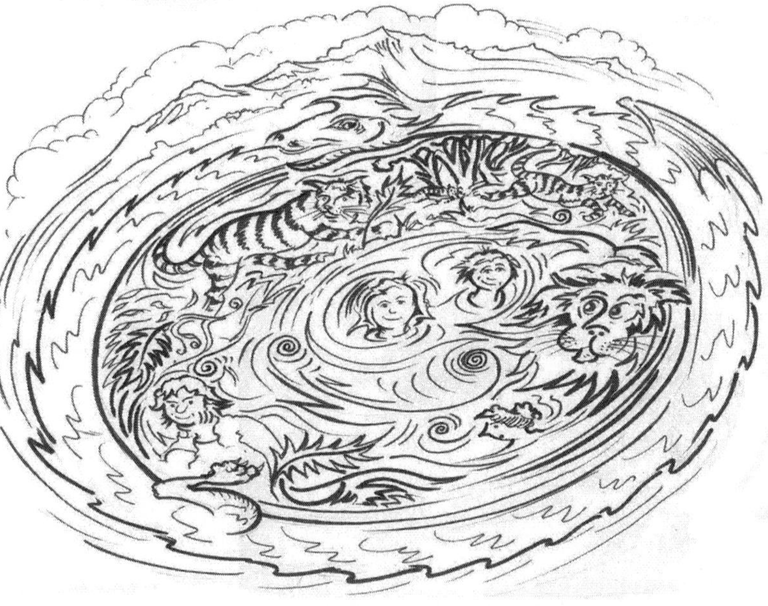

The river was shallow but no-one bothered to stop to take off their boots, they just went straight through. Everyone else started chattering, but the unity wasn't released yet.

<Still meat on kill,> was the thought that the Tesh-led unity sent after Tal. He padded away back through the forest, increasing his pace to something more normal for a tiger. Thumpus half-turned, too. Minesh, following, bumped into him.

At Tal's normal speed, it took only a few minutes to reach the kill. A fox had been gnawing at it, but ran off at the approach of the tiger. Tal settled down to chew on the delectable bones, crunching them in his powerful teeth.

'I'm me,' thought Tesh, suddenly very tired. The unity fell apart. Tal stopped chewing and raised his head. There had been animals, odd animals - a whole group of them on his territory. But they were gone now; no smell, no scent remained, except in his memory. He gave an enormous roar, to warn off any other intruders and settled back to crunching the bones again. Til had returned to her den with the cubs some time before.

The three humans who had taken part in the unity staggered. Tesh would have fallen, but Prush rushed up and held her.

<Must go further.> Thumpus who felt exhilarated, was seemingly unaffected by the experience. To be part of a tiger's consciousness was special indeed. He wouldn't have minded running back with Tal and gnawing on those bones.

'Better than rabbit!' He suppressed the thought guiltily.

The Chronicles of Thumpus Wumpus

19.

Fly like a bird

Everyone was exhausted. But, following Thumpus' advice, people struggled on. Thumpus carried children in turn. After a while, the vegetation seemed to thicken. Thumpus searched for a game track so they could get through more easily. There didn't seem to be one. He deposited Rinesh, whose turn it was to ride, and pushed through the line of bushes. Suddenly the ground fell away to cliffs dropping far down to a river, rushing hundreds of metres below. In both directions the cliffs extended at a diagonal across their track. There seemed to be no way down.

Thumpus retreated to where the rest of the tired party were sitting.

<Big drop,> he sent. <No way down. Must find tomorrow.>

Although they were not entirely out of the tigers' territory, it was time to make camp. After their experience, Suresh didn't believe that they would be attacked. The tigers had their scent connected with the experience of non-aggression, they were now far from the lair area and there seemed to be plenty of game around. They were safe enough, particularly if they kept a good fire going. No animals liked fire, apart from Thumpus, who had got used to it and now enjoyed its warmth.

They went along by the dense trees a little, till they found a gully where a small stream dropped towards the cliffs. A big fire was quickly made. They drew on their reserve supplies for supper. No-one had the energy to go searching for food.

As the evening drew in, an impromptu sharing about their experience began. Tash told how he had 'seen' the tiger cubs coming at their mother's call. After a while, all eyes turned to Tesh. She was the heroine of the day's events. But Tesh was very, very tired - too tired even to think of the words to say. She sat, trying not to keel over. Lelesh came over and wrapped her in one of the rabbit skin cloaks, cuddling her to keep her warm as she shivered with exhaustion. Thumpus came to her other side and lay down, his warm, smelly fur pressing her close. A weak little hand grabbed the fur. Lelesh unwrapped the goat-skin snug from her pack and gently stuffed Tesh into it. She did not wake, even when Thumpus and Lelesh gently moved away. Someone lent another precious skin cloak to keep her warm.

She did dream at times - of riding Tal through the forest, baring her teeth with him and roaring in a wild hunt.

Suresh was almost as tired but tried not to show it. Even Thumpus slept. When he woke, the first light of the early dawn was showing in the sky. The fire had died down. Luckily, Tal and Til had not hunted in their direction.

Thumpus, by extraordinary cunning and thought projection managed to kill three wood hares nearby. One he gulped down almost whole, giving himself indigestion. The other two he brought back to Tansh, who was stirring from sleep. He, in turn, woke Minesh. They skinned and cleaned the rabbits, revived the fire, collected some edible wild roots and leaves, and used the cook pot to make a wonderful breakfast stew. Much later, everyone else woke to its aroma.

Thumpus was keen that they didn't spend another day in the tigers' territory. He remembered images of the wall of cliffs from his mate, but she had come from the other, gentler, side, where it was easy to scan long distances for a possible way up. He explored the gully by their camp. It ended in a big drop, the stream water making rainbows as it fell to rocks at the base of the cliffs. Birds soared below him, patrolling the chasm. Feeling giddy, Thumpus backed off from the cliff edge.

At camp, Tesh was waking - the last of all. The others had restrained themselves and kept a little stew for her. She could have eaten at least twice as much. As she finished, Thumpus returned. He was overjoyed to see her awake and well, and his long wet tongue licked her face. She grabbed on to his neck. Cuddling him, she sent an image of her dream, of riding on the wild tiger's back. Thumpus growled softly and withdrew sharply, leaving Tesh a heap on the grass.

'You're jealous!' she said aloud, giggling. From a metre's distance Thumpus' dubious yellow eyes regarded her.

<Play with tiger, become meal!> he sent. Then, <Can't get down here. Must search along cliffs.> He sent a picture of the river they were camping near, of water pouring down to rocks below, of the cliff edge extending as far as one could see either side and of birds hovering in the abyss.

Tesh absorbed it. It was certainly beautiful, but how could they get down? Suddenly she had an idea.

<We don't have to. We'll find a bird and unite again. Let bird search for us. Save time and effort.>

Thumpus was uneasy. Tigers were one thing, however ferocious, but at least they had four feet on the earth. Birds were totally strange. Tesh called Suresh over.

'Thumpus says there's no way down here. I think we should unite again and love ourselves into oneness with a bird so we can search for a way. Thumpus is certain his mate came across, so a way over can't be too far.'

'Another good idea,' said Suresh. 'Let's go to the edge so we can find the right bird.'

<Not me!> sent Thumpus. <Me, ground animal. Join with Tash instead.>

<Coward!> sent Tash and Suresh together, grinning at Thumpus. He looked dejected.

<Who guide you all way? Who find you new home?>

<Oh Thumpus, you are wonderful. We'll do it with Tash.> As she spoke the words, Tesh ran up to him and grabbed both his ears, looking closely into those yellowy-brown eyes.

'First you're jealous, now you're resentful. I love you, you silly old thing!'

Thumpus didn't understand the words, but he got the meaning. He shook his head, but the girl held tight to his ears.

<Let go! Going to wump,> he sent. At that, she did let go, and he wound himself up and crashed his tail down on the ground, shaking them all. Far on the other side of their territory, Tal and Til, feeding on a fat buck, raised their heads for a moment at the boom. Thumpus felt good again. He hadn't had a proper wump for so long. But he wasn't going to join a unity with birds!

They went to the edge of the drop. It was magnificent, but scary.

'We'd better stand a good bit back,' warned Suresh. Where the gully of the little stream dropped away, they found a place where they could see into the space beyond. It was Tash who saw the bird.

'Look,' he said simply, pointing. It was a great eagle, hovering far out and above them.

'Eagles are supposed to have wonderful eyes,' said Suresh as they looked at the bird, floating on the air. 'Shall we try and connect with it?'

'Remember not to take off!' It was Tesh's joke, but they didn't laugh. Even in thought the idea of hovering on the empty air with the bird was daunting. Everyone sat down.

Then, led by Tesh, they found the beautiful unity in love, and reached out towards the eagle. Suddenly they were floating, supportless. But they had no time to enjoy the sunshine - this was hunting. This being that was part of them was at least as ferocious as Tal. Tesh allowed their unity to see with the eagle's eyes. Every part of the great cliffs was visible, far up and down the river, etched in exquisite detail by the superb eyes.

It was up river about 3 kilometres - a gap, steep but unmistakable, where a considerable tributary poured into the main river. Suddenly, before Tesh could control the thought, they were diving like a falling star, towards a tiny moving speck far below in a gap in the trees on the river's edge. They had seen a rabbit, and the eagle's appetite was tearing them out of the sky to crash to the earth below!

'I'm me-e-e!' shrieked Tash and the unity fell apart as the eagle spread its 2-metre wings in a perfect braking and adjusting movement to allow it to fall on the hapless rabbit. Tesh's breakfast came up and out. So did Tash's. Suresh was white-faced. After a while he said, 'We should have checked how hungry it was.'

Tesh reflected, 'If we had been one with it, then the fear might have destroyed its ability. What would have happened if we had crashed into the ground and it died? Would we have died too?'

'I don't know,' replied Suresh, 'and I don't propose to try it out. Well done, Tash, for getting us out in the nick of time. That quick separation you make is really important.'

Tash was recovering from his retching.

'We know where we can get down, anyway,' he said, happy at Suresh's praise. Shakily, they made their way back to the camp.

'Thumpus was right. It was much worse than Tal,' said Tesh as the others crowded around them, 'but we know where to get down. About an hour's walk up river.'

She didn't feel like sharing more right now. Tash and Suresh were silent as well. Lelesh and Prush held the two children. Even Suresh was happy to put an arm round Thumpus' neck and lean against the furry body for a moment.

<Thumpus very thin,> he sent. <Not good meal, even for Tal.>

<Very bad joke!> returned Thumpus. There wasn't anyone in the party who hadn't lost weight, but Thumpus really was skin and bones.

They made their way along the top of the cliff and then took a short detour back up the side river to find a crossing place. It would be easier to cross the main river upstream from the tributary. Then it was a scrambling, scratchy descent through scrub and brambles, down and down. Though it was warm, clouds were bubbling up over the mountains behind them. Finally, they were at the bottom, on a narrow stretch of green, the main river flowing strongly beside them.

'Let's stop for lunch,' said Tesh, very hungry.

'Good idea.' Tash agreed with her. People began putting their packs down.

<No, no, no!> sent Thumpus urgently. <Look at clouds. Must get to other bank soon.> Suresh realised what he meant.

'This area will flood if it rains hard,' he said, 'and it's going to. We've got to find a place to get over, away from the cliffs.'

Packs were re-slung over shoulders and the grumbling party moved off up river, scrambling over boulders with the rock wall towering above them. It was another hour's walk before they found a place where a huge tree, torn from the forest edge in some previous flood, had wedged in rocks, providing a precarious crossing. Big, warm raindrops were starting to fall as they inched across, one at a time, parents holding children in front of them, the dark waters racing below. The white mountain tops were now hidden in roiling black clouds.

When all were safely across, Thumpus led them well up the other bank. From there, they could see bits of broken wood and bushes caught in trees at the water's edge. The way they had walked along the other bank would be deep under water in a big flood. Up the slope was a ridge of rocks, tiny brother to the cliffs on the other side. Raindrops were falling more thickly as they scrambled into its shelter. The rocks were cracked and splintered from some past cataclysm. One huge boulder was leaning against the face of the ridge, providing shelter of a sort.

'Get bits of wood, quick!' shouted Minesh. 'It's going to pour for the rest of the day and we must have fire to dry out.' Under the big rock they gathered with armfuls of wood, huddled together as the rain began to bucket down. Great peals of thunder echoed in the mountains. Minesh got a fire going in the driest corner. They sat on their firewood and ate a damp lunch, digging deeper into their meagre supplies. There would be no hunting today.

As the day wore on, a roaring sound came from the river they had crossed. Braving the rain, which was at least warm, Tesh, Tash and some of the others made their way back down the slope. The smooth dark river had become a raging muddy torrent, carrying great tree trunks which acted like battering rams on the rocks. Of the tree they had used to cross there was no sign. The water was well up the cliffs on the other bank. If they'd stopped for lunch at the join of the rivers, they would have been swept away like straws. Thumpus' good sense had saved them.

As night fell, the storm eased; occasional, distant thunder rumbled far away. Water dribbled down the rocks. People took turns near the fire to keep the damp out and some brave individuals gathered more sodden wood, which sent clouds of steam into the air, making them cough. It was the most unpleasant night they had spent since they had left the village.

Later, it got cold as well.

The Chronicles of Thumpus Wumpus

20.

Arrival

Everyone was stiff in the morning and a bit grumpy, but the day was fair and cool. The question was, whether to stay another day, or push on. Although they had not rested properly for several days, the consensus was to go on, at least for part of the day, find a good campsite, and then rest up for a day, trying to supplement their supplies. Walking would warm everyone up, and get rid of the damp.

It wasn't difficult to find a way up the small rock ridge under which they had camped and soon they found the ground was dropping slightly; not a steep slope, but a steady one.

'We've passed the highest part,' said Suresh. If the place where Thumpus and his mate had met was halfway, they were now well on their way to their destination, wherever that was.

<Woods better here,> Thumpus added, and it was true - there was an indefinable, healthier feel. These woods were not under threat from the greedy cutters far behind them. As they walked and blood circulated once more, hope, anticipation and optimism surged back.

They stopped for a late lunch at a spot with a good stream and decided to camp. Nothing dangerous seemed to be about. They found some clearings with roots and mushrooms. Thunder rumbled around the mountains, but nothing as dramatic as the day before. The rain didn't spread to their camp.

During the next days, the euphoric mood faded. Although there were no special incidents, the forest just went on and on. The slight downhill slope continued, broken by gullies, small hills and the occasional ravine which they had to detour. Sometimes the undergrowth was thick, evidence of old forest fires. Thumpus would push through seeking the best way, but twigs snatched at clothing and scratched skin as the group followed. His coat became clogged with bits of stick and leaves. In the evenings, all the children who weren't too tired gathered around him, trying to clean the worst off his fur. Thumpus enjoyed the attention.

Another problem beset the group - boots began to give out, holes appeared in soles and uppers started to come away from them as the stitching rotted. Tansh showed people how to make a sort of moccasin from rabbit skins, but they didn't last long, particularly in the rocky areas. The weather began to get colder, particularly at night, and there was more rain. Autumn was well under way.

In addition, Thumpus, who was now a bag of bones, kept pressing the party to cut short rest breaks. He was thinking of his mate - but also of the approaching winter. He knew humans needed to have some sort of shelter and supplies before really cold weather set in.

He tried calling his mate, but there was no reply. On and on they went, food short, pace slowing, Thumpus chafing at the delays. The friendly woods now seemed drab and boring. Morale was declining. Varsh fell sick after nibbling at a root that was new to them all. Indalesh treated him with healing herbs and he slowly recovered but was weak and had to be carried a lot of the time, mainly by Thumpus. They were a sorry lot; still, they went on.

The days passed. It seemed the journey would never end. Now it was the determination of Suresh and Indalesh that led them on. Tansh and Minesh still hunted, or it would have gone hard for all. There were hardly any reserves left. Thumpus, bones sticking through fur, kept sending out messages for his mate, but still there was no reply. He gave rides to the weaker children, but it was a bony carriage.

One morning when they were at the end of their tether, Thumpus' inner ear heard what he had been hoping for - but not quite in the way he had expected. The thought he picked up was not from his mate.

<Gub, gub, gub!> It was a Thumping Wumpus thought all right, and very close indeed - only about half an hour in front of them to the right - but what did it mean?

<Heard something!> Thumpus gently disengaged himself from his small rider and was off through the forest in a flash. The rest of the party stopped in surprise.

'He heard something,' explained Tesh. 'He's gone to investigate.' People lay down where they stopped, unlacing boots if they still had them, and rubbing their aching feet. Nobody did anything at all. It was that bad.

Thumpus raced through the forest towards the source of the sound, drawing on his last energies. He did not send any thoughts, in case he would frighten away whoever it was before he could find them. Suddenly the thought was there again:

<Gub, gub, gub!>

And another, very quiet thought: <Shut up, darling brute. Give us away.>

It was Mate! Amongst the rocks over there. Yes, there was a little cave-like corner. In it, Mate and a gorgeous, cuddly, tiny Thumping, which staggered to its feet and came towards him.

<Thumpus! Been hearing you shouting days. Don't touch Thrubble! Thrubble, keep away. Big bad Thumpus eat you up!> The little ball of reddish brown fur seemed unimpressed, struggling on towards his father. Mate bared her teeth in a very unbecoming snarl and started after her cub. Thumpus hastily withdrew a few steps.

<He lovely. Never dream hurting him.> Mate was still cautious.

<Fathers not trusted with children.>

<Me different. Learnt from people. Other ways. Love Mate, love cub.>

Mate sent a big ? thought, meaning: 'Sounds interesting but I still don't trust you.' Then she lifted her head as Tesh sent a strong call:

<Thumpus? Where are you? Picking up other thoughts with yours.>

<These 'people' you shared about before. They thought-think?> sent Mate. <Why bring?>

<Three can.Great Being came. After you gone. Message. Said to bring people. My forest destroyed. We come to you.>

<How destroyed? How?> Mate sounded unbelieving. The cub cuddled at her feet. But he was looking at Thumpus.

<People like these,but different. Many. Greedy, hungry for trees. Cut, cut, cut. Never end.>

Mate shivered. <These? - not like that?>

<No. These love trees. Only take wood for dens, dropped wood for small fire keep warm.>

<Fire!> Mate's eyes were frightened.

<Very small. No fear. Keep warm. They know how. You meet now? Not dangerous. Love - Thrubble.> Thumpus was not good at new names.

<Risk - Risk. Too much.> Mate held back. Her only cub in four years. Perhaps the last Thumping Wumpus baby. She couldn't take the chance.

<Just show self. Hide baby. No risk. None,> Thumpus' thought pleaded with her.

<You bring near. I look. Thrubble stay hidden.> She raised her lip again in a snarl, to indicate that she would fight to the death if there was any advance towards Thrubble.

Thumpus didn't wait. Suddenly full of energy, he ran back through the trees.

<Come,> he sent as he arrived in sight of the bedraggled villagers. <Meet Mate.>

As Tesh translated, a faint spark of interest flickered through the group. They struggled to their feet, aching arms lifting packs once more.

'How far?' someone asked. Thumpus read the thought from many minds.

<Near, near,> Tesh explained.

It took them an hour, and there was much grumbling. It was not near at all. Finally, Thumpus sent, <Wait.>

They were near a pile of rocks. From the trees at its side, another wump emerged, slightly smaller than their own Thumpus, but in much better condition. It stood and looked at them.

<Half-dead,> it observed. <You bring *these* all the way?>

<Not half-dead. Tired from long walk,> sent Tash indignantly.

<Big cheeky cub!> Mate stared at him. Tash was furious. He was not a 'cub'! Tesh giggled and he cast her an angry glance. Then Tesh had an idea.

'Make our unity,' she said to Tash and Suresh. 'It'll save hours and hours of confusion.' Tash grimaced, but swallowed his anger and they formed the wonderful, loving, inner connection that had helped so much with tiger and eagle. Thumpus joined immediately, getting the idea, and they reached out for Mate - who held back, as the other animals could not.

<Not 'Mate'! Stupid Thumpus never even knew name! Tcharang!>

Luckily, they didn't have to try to pronounce it aloud. As they thought it, she joined them, with a sort of soft yelp. Suddenly there was also another being there, a little being, of total innocence and infinite trust. Thrubble wobbled out from behind the rocks.

'Ooh!' shouted all the other children in one voice, wide awake in an instant.

'I'm me!' said Tash quickly. As the unity broke up he continued, sending, <Can we pick him up?> All Tcharang's mistrust had gone. She looked at Thumpus, with a new fondness in her eyes.

<Safe?>

<Be gentle!> Thumpus warned Tesh, then, <Safe!> Thrubble was immediately in arms, licking faces.

<Why didn't you tell us Tch ... Tcharang's name?> Tesh asked Thumpus. Thumpus hesitated.

<Forgot,> he lied.

<Useless brute! Never even asked!> sent Tcharang, loud and clear; then, to Tesh: <All male Thumping Wumpii interested in - mating. Don't pay much attention who with!> To Thumpus, <If stay round here, big change in ways, old ruin!>

Thumpus was caught between two fires. He felt guilty because she was absolutely right. He *had* never asked her for her name. On the other hand, there was an implication in the sentence that he *could* stay round. She had that in mind. Tesh giggled. This female wump clearly stood no nonsense. She felt warm towards her.

<Can I give you a hug?> she said tentatively to Tcharang.

<First know better, then hugs,> Tcharang sent back. Tesh stepped back. Tcharang had a very different temperament to Thumpus.

<You a mess.> Tcharang had returned her attention to Thumpus. <Skin on bone. Take them to own kind, then come back, fatten up.>

Suresh, who had been listening with a smile on his face, now took her up: <Own kind? Thumpus not tell of other humans here.>

<Brown skin, but same. Not far, forest thin, then end. Few. Come and go. Not in woods. I - no attention to them.>

Suresh was really excited. Tesh also; even Tash left the crowd around Thrubble and turned to her.

<How far till forest thins?>

<Half day.> She looked at them all, lying around exhausted. <Day for you lot!>

<We'll go. We can make camp and get to the forest edge tomorrow. Is it safe?>

<Safe.>

Suresh called to the people.

'Very good news. The journey's almost over. One more day's walk. We'll go on for a bit and camp, to give Tcharang - that's Thumpus' mate's name - and Thrubble some space. Tomorrow we'll finish the journey and find a new home.'

A ragged cheer greeted his words. People stumbled up, putting on their packs a little more energetically. Only another day's walk.

<Can we come back and see Thrubble - and you?> Tash sent.

<Maybe,> returned Tcharang cautiously. But Tash was satisfied. Tcharang was just like Lelesh when she was nearly convinced. They waved. Thumpus hesitated.

<Go on. Finish job.> Tcharang licked his ear tentatively. <Then come back.>

They walked downslope for two hours and stopped for the day. It was after lunchtime anyway. A meagre meal, a desultory searching for roots and a long and disturbed sleep brought the new day. They were living on anticipation now.

As they walked on downwards in the morning sunshine, Tesh noticed the trees were changing. There were fewer big pines, more with oval, bluey-green leaves; some had autumn-coloured leaves, starting to drop. She looked back through a gap in the canopy. The white mountain was far behind, outlines fading into haze. 'It's as far away as our old home,' she thought, 'but we're lower down here.'

Legs faltering, children crying from tiredness, only supported by the thought that the journey was nearly at its end, they pressed on. At last there was a clearing, bigger than any they had passed since they left home. A stream provided water. Blackberries grew ripe.

Suresh consulted with Indalesh.

'Shall we stop here?' he asked the group. 'We could rest, recover, hunt food. Perhaps this is a good place to stay. We can explore the area, find the best site.' There was no dissent.

After that last day's walk, the first celebration was sleep. Then a pool in the stream became a bathing place. People looked at the faraway mountain, shimmering hazy white in the late afternoon sunshine and wondered, 'So far! How did we do it?'

Minesh and Tansh were hunting. There seemed to be an abundance of roots and plants, some of which no-one knew. Wild bees were around, promising honey. It was a good place. Indalesh suggested a celebration that evening.

<Watch out!> sent Thumpus suddenly. <Something coming. More than one. Know we here.> He vanished amongst the trees in an instant. The people jumped up, their lazy delight at journey's end forgotten.

'Back to the edge of the trees!' shouted Suresh. 'Grab your packs!' Half-undressed people grabbed their clothes and packs, things spilling from them, and retreated to the edge of the space.

As they did so, humans entered the clearing. Humans with sharpened hunting sticks similar to their own. Humans with almost no clothes on at all. Humans with dark brown skins. Humans talking words no-one could understand. But Tesh could.

'Many thoughts - about people stopping on their land, not from their tribe,' she whispered.

The two groups faced each other, 20 metres between them. The people held their hunting sticks, the newcomers theirs, both groups ready for trouble. A man stepped forward a pace from the brown-skinned group and said something completely unintelligible to them. Suresh stepped a pace forward too.

'We come in peace after walking five moons through the forest,' he said. The strange people shook their heads.

Tesh said excitedly, 'There's one of them who can thought-read. He picked up our thoughts. I picked up his. Let me try and connect.' Suresh nodded and himself started to listen inwardly, as did Tash.

<We're peaceful,> sent Tesh. <We've been on a long journey. We need rest.> A slim young boy at the front of the group lifted his head. *He* was the one. He turned and talked to two or three of the adults.

<Are you ghosts? Spirits? You've got the wrong skin!> he sent back.

<We're not ghosts, we're people! We've got the right skin. Are you painted?> returned Tesh.

<We've got proper skin! Is yours proper skin?>

Tesh realised that these people simply had brown skins, just as her people simply had pinkish ones.

<Yes,> she sent. She had a feeling she had been here before. Suddenly she turned excitedly to Indalesh.

'I had a dream in which I saw this scene. It said that we would be allowed to stay here if we asked with respect.'

Indalesh nodded.

'Send thoughts for me,' she said and stepped forward, beckoning Suresh. 'May we speak to your elders, please?' Tesh sent the thoughts to the boy, and, after consultation, two imposing men with white beards came to the front of the other group.

'We can speak through those who are thought-senders,' Indalesh continued, Tesh projecting the thought and translating the reply in the strange language from the thought of the young boy opposite.

<Why are you here? Where are you from? What do you want?>

<We have travelled five moons from the other side of the mountain,> translated Tesh. <We care for the forest and the land we lived in, but it is being destroyed by stupid, greedy people who are more powerful than us. We have come to find a new home. There are no more of us. We come in peace. We acknowledge that you are the custodians of this land. With deep respect we ask for your generosity to allow us to live on a small part of it.>

Remembering what Tcharang had said, she added, <We are not wanderers. We wish only to have a small area where we can build our houses and grow crops. Once our crops are growing, we will be happy to share any surplus with you. Perhaps there are skills we could exchange together.>

It was a long speech, but Indalesh spoke slowly, Suresh nodding by her side. Tesh sent it to the boy, sentence by sentence. The boy spoke at some length with the elders, who turned to the whole group. Tesh and Suresh knew he had received it clearly.

<We need time to discuss this,> the message eventually came back. <We will not harm you. Please return to your fire.>

Indalesh and Suresh motioned the people and they returned to their dying fire, closely scrutinised by the other party, who then retired to the other side of the clearing, some hundreds of metres away.

After a short discussion, the two older men and the boy returned once more and Indalesh and Suresh stood up.

<Our band has talked together,> said the elders, via the boy and Tesh. <We appreciate very much your attitude of respect for our land. We will give you permission to stay. However, the matter must go to our tribal gathering. You can come

there in due course. If all has gone well in the meantime, there will surely be no problem.>

As the people heard these words, there were shouts of joy. Their long journey was over.

Thumpus deceived a rabbit so that it ran right into his jaws. Then he raced back the way they had come. He had done his job with the people for the moment. Now it was time to be with Tcharang and Thrubble.

Suddenly the Great Being was there, green scales shining with incandescence.

<Well done,> it sent simply, looking down with a love that made Thumpus' legs collapse under him. Then it melted away. After a while, Thumpus got up shakily and went on through the forest. He would have thumped, but he didn't have the energy.

<Gub, gub, gub!> Thrubble was sending, not far away.

4740892R00096

Printed in Great Britain
by Amazon.co.uk, Ltd.,
Marston Gate.